The screams died slowly

"It's all over," said the voice above them on the bridge. "Look at them, all burned to death."

Gadgets pulled a phosphorous grenade from his battle rig. He whispered to Blancanales, "My last one."

"Make it a good throw. No rebound."

Gadgets jerked the pin, held down the lever. He took three steps, then turned and looked up at the gathered bikers.

"Hi guys," he said. He lobbed the white phosphorous and jumped back under cover.

White molten metal showered everywhere. There was screaming. Falling bikes. Exploding gas tanks. Hundreds of droplets of phosphorous seared through to bone.

Blancanales held his radio to his mouth. "Lyons, come in. Lyons! Lyons!"

No answer.

Just the smell of smoke and death.

ABLE TEAM

ABLE TEAM

AN EXECUTIONER SERIES

The Hostaged Island

Don Pendleton & Dick Stivers

A GOLD EAGLE BOOK FROM

WORLDWIDE

TORONTO • NEW YORK • LOS ANGELES • LONDON

First edition June 1982

ISBN 0-373-61202-8

Special thanks and acknowledgment to Norman Winski
and L.R. Payne for their contributions to this work.

Printed in Canada

Again, to those citizens who may
suddenly find themselves warriors in
defense of family, friends and neighbors,
this book is dedicated.

Carl Lyons: blond blue-eyed ex-LAPD sergeant, this recent veteran of the Justice Department's war against organized crime has seen enough blow-torched, pliers-mangled corpses to know what to do about today's psycho punks—shoot first.

Rosario Blancanales: from a Chicano background, he's known as Pol for Politician. Able Team's broad-shouldered senior member now fights the war against international terrorism with a special kind of sophistication and fury.

Herman Schwarz: code-named Gadgets for his wizardry with electronic devices, this Vietnam vet with metaphysical leanings has a genius-level IQ and a penchant for the unusual and unexpected in strategy and action.

1

Blood sprayed into the night.

The watchman's body twisted in his hold as he pulled the eight-inch blade of the Bowie knife across the old man's throat, severing the arteries, veins, and the windpipe. He jerked the knife back hard, felt the blade scrape the old man's vertebrae.

Horse Delaney let the dying watchman fall. Cool and cruel with heroin—he'd fixed only ten minutes before—Horse stood grinning over the old man. The watchman tried to reach his gaping throat, then died.

The red-bearded, long-haired biker wiped the Bowie knife on his greasy jeans and slipped it into the sheath on his belt. He took a last glance around the docks.

To his right, the truck ramp led to the moorings of a tug boat and cargo barge. The barge carried four semitrailers bound for the markets, restaurants, and shops of Santa Catalina Island. Beyond the docks, ship lights and pilot beacons streaked the oil-black water of Wilmington Harbor.

To his left, an area of asphalt separated the docks from the warehouses. Tractor trailers were parked there, with stacked pallets of cargo alongside of them. Mercury-arc streetlights cast a bluish glare, yet left the alleys separating the warehouses in complete darkness.

Taking his hand-radio from the pocket of his denim jacket, Horse pressed the "transmit" button.

"It's clear, move it."

Six men in dênim and leather ran from the sha-dowed alleys; two men from the alley directly op-posite Horse, two from each of the alleys to the north and south. They carried assault rifles. The two pairs of men to the north and south slipped into shadows a hundred yards from where Horse stood. They leaned back against alley walls as if to melt into them. They were on the lookout.

The two men from the center alley ran directly to Horse. Charlie, a lean biker with a lot of kinky blond hair and no front teeth, carried Horse's gear: govern-ment .45 with ten magazines on a military web belt, .45 MAC-10 fitted with suppressor, a bandolier carry-ing ten 30-round magazines for the MAC-10. Horse buckled the web belt and slipped on the bandolier.

He turned to the second man, the full-blooded Navajo with his Mohawk haircut who looked like a bird of prey.

"Chief, bring in the trucks."

The hooked-nose Indian, scowling, raised his hand-radio to his mouth. In seconds they heard the muffled rumble of diesel engines. As the first stolen semitrailer emerged from the alley:

"Chief! Guide them around. Charlie, get that—" Horse glanced at the dead watchman "—thing out of the way. We hafta take him out a couple of miles before we dump him. We can't have someone find him, can't have nothing go wrong."

The first semi wheeled in an arc, then backed up to the loading ramp. Chief yanked open the trailer's doors. Bikers jumped to the asphalt, pulled long planks from inside the trailer. Even as Chief guided the second semi to its place alongside the first, silent bikers wheeled their Kawasakis, Harleys, Suzukis and Hondas out of the trailer. Then more of them descended from the second trailer.

They wore denim jeans and black leather jackets studded with chrome, steel-toed motorcycle boots, Nazi helmets, Confederate caps, even Stetsons. They all carried weapons: assault rifles, submachine guns, revolvers, pistols, knives, machetes. On the back of every jacket was a grinning skull winged with flames—The Outlaws. All of them were male.

"Line the bikes up!" yelled Horse, pacing the loading ramp. "Over there, line them over there. Keep this ramp clear. Chief! Form everyone up. Charlie, break the locks off those trailers on the boat. Where's Turk? Turk!"

"Something wrong?" The dull-eyed ex-merchant marine ambled up to Horse. Turk was a balding giant with thick features, huge arms and shoulders falling about his beer belly. His ten-shot pistol-grip Ithaca riot shotgun hung in front of him, the sling looped behind his neck, his hands folded over the receiver.

"You know your job. Get in that tug, get that engine going."

"Ah, yeah. Was just gonna do that—"

"Three minutes! Three minutes and then we're on our way."

Aboard the barge, Charlie began to throw the boxes and crates from the interior of a semitrailer to the bikers on the dock. A line of bikers passed the freight from the dock, hand-to-hand up the loading ramp at the back of the semitrailer on land. As the last of the motorcycles came down the plank ramps, bikers threw the freight into the empty trailer.

Other bikers unloaded the gang's heavy weapons from the second semitrailer. It had taken the Outlaws months to assemble the contents of these nylon and oilskin cases. They had looted gun-shops, burglarized the homes of collectors, traded drugs for what they could not buy: M-60 machine guns, Marlin .444s with telescopic sights, grenades. A raid on the desert bunker of a radical Christian sect gained LAAW (Light Anti-Armor Weapon) rockets still in cases marked for shipment to Korea, .50 caliber Browning machine guns, and light mortars. It had taken three pickup trucks to carry away the weapons and ammunition. Now the weapons were bound for Santa Catalina Island.

Horse watched the unloading of the weapons, then spoke into his hand-radio:

"Anybody see anything?"

Two voices answered simultaneously. Horse jabbed the "transmit": "One at a time. Jake, what're you talking about?"

"Nothing. Nobody. The docks ain't the place for a big Saturday night. You want us to come in?"

"No! Stay there. Now you, Bart. What's—"

"Zero." The voice from the radio slurred the word as if half-asleep. "It's just dark and peaceful. What a trip, man. Just us and the rats."

"Pete, you there?" Horse called for the man watching the far side of the warehouses.

"I'm here. Watching everything. There's nothing to see."

"Stay there, all of you, a few more minutes."

The tug's engine sputtered, then revved. Clouds of diesel smoke burst from its stack. Turk leaned from the cabin and waved to the mass of men on the dock. Then he spotted Horse, went back to his job. The diesels' sputterings and pops smoothed to a steady, almost inaudible background idle.

Several bikers heaved the planks to the barge. As the first of the chromed and lacquered motorcycles went into the one emptied trailer, Charlie broke the locks off the second one. Horse strode down the ramp.

"What's taking you so long? Get that trash out of there!"

Toothless Charlie glanced at his watch, but he didn't pause as he passed box after box to the human conveyor belt below him. "We're thirty seconds ahead of schedule," he said. "Be cool, Horse. Why don't you take a break, maybe a little skullpop for you? Your nerves—"

Horse's MAC-10 pointed at Charlie's face. Charlie looked down the .45 caliber hole in the suppressor, continued unloading. "I'm just doing my work, Horse. Working as fast as I can. Can't work if I'm dead."

"Then you don't tell me what to do. I tell *you*." Horse stomped back up the ramp, past the rows of bikes, pushing through the groups of sweating Outlaws. He surveyed the scene. There was nothing more he could do. They all knew their jobs.

He went to the far side of the trucks. He was alone

there. He leaned against the semi's radiator, watching the alleys and warehouses for movement. Nothing. He wished someone would appear. A guard, a dockworker, a warehouse manager. Anyone. He'd already killed twice tonight: a black teenage security guard, studying some textbook in the guard shack, and then the old man. Another kill would be almost as good as heroin. Almost. Nothing was quite as good as heroin. Not killing, not fucking, not highway cruising. And after tonight, he'd never have to hustle again; he'd be rich, super-rich.

Fifteen years ago he had walked away from San Quentin after two years inside for the theft of a motorcycle. It made him laugh. As a teenager he had committed assault, rape, murder, mayhem, but they put him away for breaking a showroom window and riding off on a Harley. Since then he had never done anything so paltry.

First he formed the Outlaws. With this gang of psychos and misfits, he pretty soon whipped the other motorcycle outfits into line.

They took on the West Coast syndicate for the control of the heroin trade in San Bernardino County, and they won. Then they took a big piece of the Los Angeles trade from the black and Chicano gangs.

But tonight was different. Tonight was not some gang war for a few thousand dollars a week in heroin profits.

Tonight would be for millions.

As the tug and barges left Wilmington Harbor, Chief scanned the water and the lights behind them from the pilot's cabin. Nothing moved on the dark breakwater. No Coast Guard craft pursued them. No flashing lights from Police or Harbor Master. He lifted the binoculars to his eyes, tried to find the truck docks in the dark mass of wharves and warehouses along the shore. He couldn't see the dock. He buzzed Horse on the hand-radio:

"We're out of the harbor."

"Anything following us?"

"Nah."

Horse pocketed his radio and turned to the other Outlaws in the trailer with him. "We're on our way."

The fifty-odd bikers were packed shoulder-to-shoulder in the tangle of motorcycles and weapons. They cheered, shoving into one another. Some beat their fists on the aluminum sheeting of the trailer. Horse stepped up on a customized chopped Harley, raised his arms for order:

"Shut the fuck up! Trailers full of tomatoes and soda pop don't scream, remember? You want to come this far and get busted? QUIET!"

The trailer fell silent. From the second trailer beside them on the barge, they heard the cheering of the twenty other Outlaws. Horse pulled out the hand-radio and hissed:

"Charlie! Shut them up! Now!"

"Sure, boss. Can we smoke now?"

"No smoking."

"Not even tobacco? I'm having a nicotine fit."

"Cigarettes okay. But no grass, no PCP. And no lights, no cigarettes once we start unloading. You know the plan."

Then he glared at the Outlaws in front of him.

"You heard what I told Charlie. Everyone stays straight until we take the Island. No one leaves the trailers until we dock.

"No cigarettes, no noise, no shooting. Only knives. Me and the guys with silencers will do any shooting. You see one of the Catalina pigs and you don't have a silencer, you let him go. No noise, no alarms, nothing! Understand?"

The bikers murmured their compliance. But one of them, Stonewall, the one in the Confederate cap, raised his parkerized Remington 870. The riot weapon had been modified with a magazine extension and a bayonet mount.

"When we start the round-up," Stonewall asked, "what happens if the locals—"

"If the locals don't follow orders, they die. Once the round-up starts, anything that doesn't move when it's told to, dies. Tell them once, then kill them. But that's only after the special squads are in position. Silence until we turn on the sirens. Then it's straight ahead and we don't stop until the island is ours."

Horse raised his arms to quiet the cheer.

"Remember this," he commanded. "We stay together, everyone does his job, we can't lose. But if anyone pulls some chicken shit trick, anyone gets in a hard place and thinks he can surrender, you think about what I'm going to tell you now.

"We killed four guards to get to the docks. We killed those crazy Jesus-people out in the desert. And we're gonna kill every last hero that tries to stop us on the island. That's murder-by-ambush, that's conspiracy-to-murder, that's murder of witnesses. That's mandatory death sentence, for all of us.

"Some chicken shit thinks he's going to bargain his way out of anything, the most he can hope for is life. Life in a little concrete room. I been inside, I know. So do the chicken shit a favor and kill him. Do us all a favor, kill him. Do we all understand!"

Horse let the bikers cheer and shout. "Outlaws forever!" they yelled. He pushed open the trailer door and jumped down to the barge deck. He stood at the barge's safety ropes for a minute, watching the lights of the Harbor and Long Beach recede.

Then he went into the second trailer. There he answered the questions of twenty more Outlaws, gave them the same speech as the first group. Same seething threats, same encouragement, same venom.

The voices of seventy-two Outlaws had faded, and Horse needed a fix. He wandered the deck of the barge, found shelter from the wind and salt-spray behind the wheels of a semitrailer, and unwrapped his kit. He heard the shuffling of heavy boots above him as he cooked the heroin with the flame of his butane lighter. He pushed up the sleeve of his jacket, tied off, found a vein under all the scars. Horse had been an addict for the past ten years, his habit costing him hundreds of dollars a day. The rush still lifted him to heaven.

His brain floating, Horse watched the wake of the tug and cargo barge churn the dark ocean. He had been a child and teenager on Catalina. The people had beaten him, jailed him, humiliated him, driven him out of their precious community.

Now he returned.

He returned with a gang of seventy-two felons, psychopaths, addicts.

He came back with a Plan. A lethal plan conceived and drafted by the only man Horse had ever admired: an ally, a friend, and a man of wealth and prestige and position.

He came back with a white-hot hatred for the community that had rejected him. The people of the island would suffer the terror of the Outlaws. The people would die. And their terror and death would make Horse rich beyond his dreams.

2

Fearful of a Japanese invasion of California during World War II, the United States Maritime Service had turned Catalina Island into a fortress and training ground for the armed services.

Closed to the public throughout the war years, only a few civilians had remained on Catalina. Submarines, aircraft carriers and battleships crowded the waters beyond Avalon Bay and Two-Harbors on the island's isthmus. Units from every branch of the armed forces trained on the island. As part of the military presence, the Maritime Service installed a network of loudspeakers and air-raid sirens throughout the city of Avalon.

With the end of the Second World War and the dismantling of the military installations, the network of speakers and sirens remained, intact and periodically tested, as part of the Civil Defense program, in case of another global conflict or the threat of disaster.

Now, suddenly, the sirens ripped the silence of sleeping Avalon.

The people awoke confused. Why would the Civil Defense authorities alert them at two-thirty Sunday morning?

What was it? A tidal wave? Nuclear war? A drowning movie star?

Thoughts both of catastrophe and absurdity raced through the sleepy minds of the islanders as the men, women and children forced themselves to leave homes on the streets and hillsides of Avalon and dutifully brave the chill air. Neighbors gathered in the night in groups, questioning one another. No one had answers.

"Wow, man," Jack Webster smiled, blowing smoke at the ceiling. "It's the end of the world. It's the big Number Three. It's a super-nuke, coming down at ten thousand miles an hour. It's got my name on it!" He took another long drag on the hand-rolled cigarette, exhaling marijuana smoke. "There I go, up in smoke."

Chris Davis laughed, leaning back in the overstuffed chair. He turned on the radio. "That isn't the way it is. All nukes are addressed 'To Whom It May Concern.' You, me, all of us."

"Tell me about it, college boy," Jack muttered lazily.

Chris spun the radio dial, passed several mainland stations. He found the frequency he wanted, but there was only static. "Hey, there's nothing on KCAT."

"There's never anything on KCAT."

"It's just noise. Listen. What's going on, I wonder?" Christ tuned in one of the Los Angeles news stations. The announcer droned on with the standard bad news. "Nothing special on the mainland stations. . . ."

Another young man, Roger Davis, went to the window of the garage apartment that he shared with

Chris. They were cousins, and Roger had the same wide surfer-shoulders as Chris, and almost the same features and long-limbed build. But he had a tan that Chris would never equal. Roger was a mulatto teenager the color of coffee with cream. His tightly curling hair was an almost orange blond.

Hanging his head out the window, he could look down the driveway, past his aunt and uncle's house, to the street. He saw groups of people milling about, talking.

"All the old folks are out there," he told Chris and Jack. He took the joint from Jack, pulled down a hit. Then he picked up the telephone. "I'll call the other guys. Hey, the phone's dead."

"What *is* going on?" Chris went to the window.

With startling clarity, a voice sounded over the Civil Defense public address system, silencing everybody. "This is an emergency. Repeat, emergency. All residents assemble on the beach. All residents assemble on the beach as quickly as possible. Do not stop for anything. Your lives depend on moving quickly. Repeat, this is an emergency."

"Who's that?" Roger asked.

"It isn't the sheriff. That's not his voice," said Chris. "Let's get moving, maybe mom and dad will need help."

"Let Sheriff Fletcher help them," Jack blurted. "We help ourselves. With everyone down on the beach, we can take whatever we want. We could get a whole mountain of loot. We could be set for years!"

"What are you talking about?" said Roger.

"You can forget that," Chris glared at Jack. "The law says looters get shot."

"He goes to college and he thinks he's a lawyer," Jack sneered. "Who's going to see us? It's dark out there. It'll be like Watts. Everybody gets a color TV."

Glen Shepard riffled through his wife's closet in search of a maternity dress. Ann waited, sitting on the edge of the bed, eight months pregnant. She picked up the bedside phone, dialed, listened. She clicked the receiver several times.

"Come on, stand up, let's get some clothes on the sleepwalker."

"The phone isn't working."

"Lines are probably jammed. Everyone calling at once."

"No, there's no tone at all."

"Arms up." He dropped the dress over her head, guiding it over her shoulders. "I'll go find out what's going on, but you've got to be ready to move."

"Why? If it's war, we're in the best place we can be. And if it isn't, there's nothing anyone—"

"Just turn on the radio," Glen cajoled his wife, his voice soothing. Anemic because of her pregnancy, she had not worke in weeks. She had stayed in the house, slept, and if awake had alternated between boredom and bad-temper. "I'll be back from the beach in a few minutes. I saw everyone on the block go down that way ten minutes ago."

They heard heavy boots on the porch. Their dog, a year-old Rotweiller, ran from the back of the house and barked a challenge.

"I'll see who it is," Glen told her. He walked quickly through the house. He pushed aside the front curtains.

"Who's there?"

"Get to the beach! This is an emergency."

Glen switched off the living room lights, simultaneously flicking on the porch light. He saw a bearded, leather-jacketed man in a chromed Nazi helmet. He saw the longhair swinging a short-barreled shotgun toward him.

Even as he stumbled back, the door exploded in front of Glen, the lock and knob and door jam disintegrating. Glen fell backward, and tumbled to the floor.

The man kicked the door open, saw the dog, fired again. The blast took away the dog's foreleg at the shoulder. The yelping animal rebounded from the wall and, in crazed rage, leaped at the man. The gun blasted again, and the dog's head disappeared in a red splash. The gunman stepped over the twitching remains and pointed the sawed-off barrel at Glen's face.

"Up, motherfucker! Out on the street! Who else is in here?" The biker stepped past Glen, started toward the bedroom.

"NO!" Glen screamed, lunging up from the floor. He grabbed the weapon with both hands, trying to twist it away. The biker kneed him in the stomach. Then he whipped the shotgun's stock into Glen's face.

Blood and broken teeth sprayed from the householder's mouth. Glen attacked again. The bearded man grinned and kicked Glen in the stomach with vicious force, slamming him back against the wall.

"Okay, hero. Die."

Glen twisted away as the biker fired once more.

Pellets slashed his back. He scrambled across the floor on his hands and knees. There was another blast behind him, then another and another. It was the biker who fell hard, groaning.

Ann stood in the doorway, their Smith and Wesson .357 Magnum in her hands, the Model 13's four-inch barrel still smoking.

A voice called from the street. "What's going on in there? Bull!"

Blood foamed from the mouth of the longhair on the floor.

Glen saw him try to grasp a pistol in a shoulder holster, trying to get a hold on it inside his jacket. Glen grabbed the shotgun from the floor. He pointed it at the man's head and pulled the trigger. Nothing. He pumped the slide, heard the hammer click. Empty.

As the biker finally pulled the pistol from the holster, Glen swung the shotgun like a club and smashed the man's head. He brought down the shotgun three times.

A gun blast outside sent slugs ripping through the house. "Down, Ann!" screamed Glen. The words felt strange coming from his numb, shattered mouth. Then he crawled again, kicked the front door closed, dragged the couch across the doorway. Glass and plaster fell around him as more bullets punched through the house.

"Glen, where are you?" Ann screamed.

"I'm okay, I'm okay. Lie down on the floor. Go back to the bedroom."

He crawled back to the dying biker. The man still breathed. Glen found his revolver, a snub-nosed

stainless steel Colt Lawman. He put the pistol in his
pants pocket. He searched through the man's jacket
pockets, finding speed-loaders and a box of cartridges. He unbuckled the nylon bandolier of shotgun cartridges from the man's waist, then he took the
bloody shotgun and crawled out of the living room.

Ann lay on the bedroom floor. The Smith and
Wesson was still firmly in her grip. Her swollen
breasts rose and fell with deep, slow breathing.

"What's wrong?" he asked. "Is the baby—"

"What's wrong? Someone's shooting at us! I'm
trying to stay calm. Did I kill him?"

"Not quite—"

She was pissed. Pregnant and pouting, she cursed
the biker. "I can't stand this— Oh, God! Your face,
you're—"

"I can get new teeth. Now we have to get out."

"What's happening out there? Where can we go?"

Glen threw open the back window. "Away from
here. Let's go."

"Mom! Dad! You here?" Chris Davis walked
through his parents' home, calling out. No one
answered. He glanced into the bedroom. A commer-
cial jingle prattled from the bedside clock-radio. He
went to the living room and saw the front door standing open. He looked outside. The street was empty.

"They here?" his cousin Roger called from the
kitchen.

"No."

Gunshots boomed through the night. Jack Webster raced in through the kitchen door. "Someone's
shooting on the other side of the block!"

"Christ. A shotgun." Chris locked and chained the front door. He hurried through the house, turning off all the lights, checking the windows and patio doors.

"Still want to go looting?" he cried at Jack as they passed each other.

There were more shots a few blocks away, toward the beach. The youths looked at each other, words failing them. Then a strange scream came from the street. It rose and fell; it wasn't a scream of fright, it was like a rebel yell. It ended in a crackle of mad laughter and the roar of a motorcycle engine.

The three teens heard the sound of their surfboards fall. They had leaned the boards against the back fence. Someone was coming in through the back.

The house was dark. Chris felt his way to his father's study. Roger and Jack were only a step behind him. Chris didn't risk turning on the lights.

"Gimme the lighter, Jack."

By the flame's soft glow, Chris found the second drawer of his father's desk, pulled it out, found the key taped to the underside. It was the spare key to the gun closet.

From the closet he removed the long-barreled semi-automatic 12-gauge that his father had used to win second place in Catalina's trap shooting tournament. Also the double-barreled 12-gauge that his dad took hunting. He passed the double-barreled weapon to his cousin Roger.

"What do I get?" Jack protested. "I've got to have—"

"Here." Chris passed him a holstered pistol.

"An automatic. Wow. What about ammunition?"

"In those pouches on the belt." Chris found a day pack in the closet drawers, hastily dumped boxes and boxes of 12-gauge shells in the pack.

The back door screen rattled. Chris fed shells into the long shotgun's magazine. He passed a handful of shells to Roger.

Jack struggled to fasten the gun belt around his waist as he walked to the kitchen. Once there, he unsnapped the holster flap, took out the Colt .45, pointed it at the shadow on the kitchen door and pulled the trigger, even as Chris smashed the pistol down.

"You jerk-off!" Chris hissed. "We don't know who's out there. Anyway, you have to cock an automatic." Chris worked the shotgun's action, calling out in a loud voice: "Who's out there? Identify yourself or I'll fire!"

"Don't shoot—" a woman pleaded.

"It's Glen Shepard, from the other street—"

"That's the political freak, the guy with all the bumper stickers," Jack said.

"Please let us in," said a male voice. "My wife's pregnant—"

Roger opened the door. Even in the semi-darkness, the curly-haired boy had to turn away when he saw Glen Shepard. Glistening blood covered his face and chest. There was blood on his hands up to his elbows. His pregnant wife was smeared with it.

"God, what happened?" Chris asked.

Glen helped Ann to a chair. "A hoodlum shot his way into our house," said Glen, gasping for breath. In the window's light, they saw that most of his teeth were gone. "Ann gunned him down. Then a bunch of them started shooting at the house—"

"We've got to call the sheriff." Roger went to the kitchen's wall phone and dialed in nervous desperation. He clicked the receiver twice.

"Nothing, right?" Glen asked.

"The line's dead."

Outside, shots popped in the distance. More shots burst out on the other side of the block. Glen took a dishrag from the sink and wiped off the bloodied shotgun he was carrying.

"I think it's up to us to help ourselves," he muttered.

3

Islanders in robes, pajamas, casual clothes crowded the wide walkway that paralleled the beach. Family groups and clusters of neighbors waited for official explanation of this emergency assembly. The sirens were wailing again. It was ten minutes since they had heard the voice over the loudspeakers.

Babies cried; children ran through the cold tide-soaked sand, parents calling after them. Friends talked and waved to each other and introduced neighbors. Islanders continued to stroll down from the residential areas. In twos and threes they joined the mass of people already on the beach. They too talked animatedly with their neighbors as they walked.

One man on the beach—stocky, his short hair sticking up in various directions—limped from group to group, always questioning. People shrugged, shook their heads.

Then he went in to one of the tourist hotels, The Pavilion Lodge.

"Hey, Max!" The desk clerk called out to the limping man as he crossed the lobby. "You talked to the sheriff yet?"

"Can't find him anywhere," Max said. "I been up and down the beach. Haven't talked to anyone who has seen him, either."

"Christ, just what we need," the clerk complained. "A weekend crowd in the hotel and we get an emergency I can't even explain."

"Pass out the complimentary booze," Max smiled. He was almost an old-timer on the island. "Keep them pacified." Despite the lobby's warmth, he kept his coat closed. He was shivering. He wore a sports coat, slacks, a pinstripe shirt with a tie, shined shoes: Max was a traveling salesman accustomed to dressing quickly.

"Not that easy," the clerk told him. The balding man leaned across his desk, spoke quietly. "I got some people here—the reservation came on a fancy corporate letterhead, they pay with corporate checks, but they've got two Secret Service agents with them. I can tell. These big guys in gray suits, nasty metal things with handles on them right here—" the clerk reached for his left armpit. "—you get the picture. They ask me what's going on, I can't tell them. They look at me like I'm dog shit on their shoe."

"Do you really think they're Secret Service?" Max had studied all the guests in the lobby. He saw one wide-shouldered young man with a briefcase in his hands, stationed in front of the door leading to the hotel's party lounge, who looked like he was on a military field, standing at parade rest.

The clerk pointed at his lapel. "They got these little buttons—and anyway, the sheriff told me. There's two of them with these six professor types. Why did all this have to happen this weekend?"

Max stared hard at the young Secret Service agent, then he turned and without a word limped quickly out of the hotel. As he did so, there was the nearby sound of automatic weapon fire.

"Mayday, Mayday!" the officer chanted into the shortwave radio's microphone. "This is Deputy Sheriff Fletcher of the Avalon Sheriff's Office on Santa Catalina Island. We are under attack by an armed motorcycle gang. We are under attack by an armed motorcycle gang. They have automatic weapons. They have killed several residents. They are taking hostages.

"Mayday, Mayday. Please, anyone hearing this call, notify the mainland. We are under attack—"

The young deputy heard motorcycles, then voices. The glass of the office's front door shattered.

"Mayday, Mayday. This is Santa Catalina Island. We are under attack by a motorcycle gang. They are killing—"

Shotgun blasts rocked the outer office. As he spoke into the microphone, the deputy took out his speed-loaders and laid them on the table in front of him. Then he cocked his .38 service revolver and aimed it at the closed inner office door. He heard the front door being kicked open. He heard the sickening shock of rifle fire and shotgun blasts. Slugs punched through the office wall.

"—This is the Avalon Sheriff's Office! We are under attack by a motorcycle gang. Contact the mainland. All communications here are dead. Please contact the—"

Sections of the wall exploded inward. Plaster, framed photos and certificates, books flew through the office. Deputy Fletcher felt a slug rip across the top of his thigh. He fired his .38 at the door. The pistol made only a pop-pop-pop against the noise and chaos.

Then a shock literally threw him against the radio.

As he lost consciousness, he raised his pistol to fire at the silhouette in the doorway.

Howling and laughing, the Outlaws swept down from the hills, islanders sprinting in panic before them. The bikers fired their weapons into the night sky as they herded groups of residents to the beach. Forming bike lines of chrome and steel where the side streets met the beach walkway, they blocked any escape.

From the south, a line of Outlaws pushed the crowd toward the old Casino. Shouting commands, firing weapons over the heads of their prisoners, the bikers rode handlebar to handlebar. Other men on motorcycles criss-crossed the beach, their wheels throwing sprays of sand and salt water, cutting off the few islanders who had attempted to dash to small boats moored only a few yards offshore in the calm bay.

Gang members ordered the tourists from the hotel lobbies, then searched the rooms. Those who attempted to hide, or who struggled when they were dragged out, suffered a kick in the groin and a smash over the head from a gun butt.

Max limped beside his wife and teenage daughter. He watched for a chance to break free. He had lived on the island for the fifteen years since his discharge from the army. He knew every shop, every doorway, every alley. He pulled his wife Carol and his daughter Julia close to him and said:

"We're going to slip away from here. Move over toward the shops as we walk—"

"You can't outrun them," his wife told him. "You try and—"

"I know I can't run. That little alley beside Jim Peterson's restaurant? The lock on the gate is broken.... You push on it, it opens. We're going to duck into that alley, close the gate behind us. We'll hide back there."

"You have your gun?" Carol asked him.

Max pressed his coat. There was the outline of an auto-pistol. "You ready?" he asked. Carol nodded. "And you, Julia?"

His daughter clutched his arm and nodded. They pushed through the mob of terror-stricken friends and neighbors. The restaurant was three doors ahead of them.

"One more thing," Max told them. "Nobody comes with us. Now move fast."

They passed the restaurant. Max took a last look around, then shoved his wife and daughter ahead of him, knocking the iron grill open with the force of their bodies. In an instant he kicked the gate closed behind them. Then he pushed them into the shadows.

A bare bulb lit the narrow alley. Max found a bottle and gently smacked the bulb.

The alley went dark. He slipped the Colt Hardballer from his belt. "Let's go," he whispered.

He led them down the alley. Behind them passed a line of men on motorcycles, screaming and howling and laughing, like something from a nightmare.

Max led his wife and daughter around a corner. Here, the alley passed behind the Pavillion Lodge. Someone moved in the hotel's service entry. Instinctively, the three of them took cover.

It was the Secret Service agent Max had seen earlier. He held an Uzi machine-pistol. Max and his family were so close they heard footsteps on the concrete.

The agent spoke to some newcomers. "I'm point. Follow me, gentlemen." The agent led five briefcase-bearing men in suits from the doorway. At the street the agent glanced in both directions. He motioned the five men against the hotel wall.

"Where's Mr. Severine?" the agent asked the men. The five all looked at one another. The agent pointed at them. "Stay there."

Cat-silent, he returned to the doorway. He stopped short, his face going slack with surprise: "Mr. Sever—"

A point-blank pistol shot threw him back. Seeing the agent killed, the five men in suits scattered into the street. There were shouts, the roar of motorcycles, as laughing, yelling bikers saw and pursued them.

As Max watched, a sixth middle-aged man appeared. This was Severine. Like the others, he wore a conservative suit. But he also held a pistol. He walked over to the dead Secret Service agent and dropped the pistol. Then he walked calmly into the street and let the bikers take him.

Seconds later, several motorcycles roared into the alley. Damnation. The headlights had found Max, his wife, his daughter.

Built in 1909 for fishermen and the resident employees of the Wrigley Company, Catalina's Pleasure Pier now serves the tourist trade. From the pier, glass-bottom boats shuttle visitors to view the bay's kelp forests and sea life. Other boats take tourists to view the colonies of California sea lions, to cruise through the splendid isolation of Two Harbors, to watch the nightly phenomenon of flying fish leaping over the sea's surface on silver gossamer wings.

The pier holds rental shops offering motor launches, rubber rafts, and scuba gear. The restaurants there sell what many islanders and tourists swear to be the most delicious shrimp and crab cocktails on the West Coast.

The Harbor Master's office occupies the seaward end of Pleasure Pier. A simple green shack, its unimpressive exterior hides the interior's state-of-the-art electronics. Banks of radar screens, linked by cable to radar scanners on top of Catalina's second highest mountain, Mount Black Jack, monitor all marine and aircraft traffic to the mainland on the north, east, and south, and far into the Pacific Ocean to the west.

Horse pressed the muzzle of his cocked .45 automatic against the head of the duty officer in the Harbor Master's office. The young man, despite himself, shook with fear. Horse grinned as he surveyed the consoles of radar screens. He knew he could spot any police or military attempt to land forces, whether by sea or by air. He could then send his bikers to eliminate the threat.

And if the authorities mounted an overwhelming attack, the Outlaws would simply execute all the hostages, then fight to the death.

"All right!" Horse glanced at Banzai, demon-faced biker of Japanese ancestry. "You see all this? This is ours now. We got early warning!"

Banzai's hand-radio buzzed. "Yeah, what?" He listened and then reported to Horse. "They're bringing in one of the sheriffs. His name's Fletcher."

"Fletcher? Deputy pig Fletcher?" Horse laughed. He took a slip of paper from his jacket and put it in front of the duty officer. "Okay, boy, you wanna stay alive?" The young man nodded. "So I'm the main man now. You do what I say. Call this number—now."

The paper read: "Governor's Hot-line," followed by a line of numbers.

The duty officer's hands shook as he dialed. "It's—it's—" he stuttered, finally getting the words out. "It's ringing."

Horse shoved the young duty officer off the chair and took the phone. He listened to the distant ringing. Once, twice, three times. He watched the spinning green line of the radar scan sweep the screen: green blips marked the positions of stationary ships all around Catalina. Finally, after six rings:

"Hello..." A sleepy voice came from the phone. "This is the Governor...who's calling?"

"Jerry baby! This is the Outlaws' number one talking to you. You listening? I'm going to give it to you fast and only once."

"Is this some kind of joke?" The Governor's voice had come alive. "Who's calling? How'd you get this number?"

"Never mind that crap. You just listen. We got fifteen hundred hostages. We're going to kill them—are you listening?"

"What is it you want?"

"So you're listening. One, I want my three

chemists out of jail. The ones you got in jail for manufacturing a bit of PCP. That's number one.''

"Go on.''

Horse heard a click on the line. That meant the call was now monitored and recorded. ''Two, we want twenty million in gold bullion. Twenty million dollars in gold, understand? And three, you got the nuclear submarine *Orizaba* parked in San Francisco Bay. You put my men, my gold in the sub and bring it here. You've got forty-eight hours. Understand?''

Behind Horse, the door opened. Two bikers half-dragged, half-carried Deputy Sheriff Fletcher into the room.

Most of Fletcher's right hand had been shot away. Two fingers dangled from a mess of blood and exposed bones. A tourniquet cut from a telephone cord and knotted above his wrist slowed his loss of blood. His other wounds had not been treated. A gaping wound across one thigh poured blood down his slacks. There was a clear imprint of a boot heel on his face.

"How do I know this isn't a hoax?'' the Governor shouted. "You'll have to talk to my people—''

''I got a pal here for you to talk to.'' Horse turned to the deputy. "Hey, Fletcher. Remember me? During the summer? You whipped my head with your stick, remember?''

Fletcher recognized Horse through swollen eyes. But he said nothing.

"What's wrong? You too fucked up to talk? Does it hurt? Don't sweat it, I got something to make the hurt go away. Just for you. Now talk to the Governor.'' Horse pushed the handset against the deputy's face. "Tell him your name.''

"This... is Deputy Sheriff... Joseph Fletcher, of the Avalon Sheriff's Office. We are under attack by a motorcycle gang. We need...."

"Have they really taken all the people hostage?" the Governor barked down the phone.

"I don't know. They're killing people... they—"

Horse raised his .45 to the deputy sheriff's face. "I'm going to take away the hurt now, Fletcher. Say bye-bye to the Governor."

Fletcher closed his eyes. "Hail Mary, mother of grace. Forgive us our sins, now and at the time of our—"

The shot sent blood spewing over the Harbor Master's map of Santa Catalina Island.

4

Mist streaked the Virginia mountains. Defining the eastern ridgelines, the first light of day illuminated the autumn colors of the forest. The valley floor remained in darkness. Carl Lyons ran through bands of shadow and startling brilliance. He pumped his legs as if they were components of an unfeeling machine, disregarding muscle pain and rasping breath. He heard Rosario Blancanales a hundred yards below him on the mountainside. Lyons rounded a bend in the trail, took cover behind a fallen tree, waited.

As Blancanales' running steps approached, Lyons found a fist-sized clod of dirt. He continued to wait. But Blancanales didn't appear. Lyons could hear the rush and flutter of the bird's wings through the air. But he didn't hear Blancanales.

A stick hit the back of his head. Lyons spun and tumbled over. He saw smiling Blancanales squatting uphill from him.

"I thought the race was to the top of the hill." Blancanales stood, stretched. "But if you can't hack it—"

An electronic beep interrupted him. The pagers clipped to their sweatsuit waistbands beeped three times. There was a pause, then three more beeps.

Their grins faded. The morning exercise was over. Three beeps meant no more jokes.

As they sprinted down the trail, they heard overhead the heavy throbbing of a military helicopter.

April Rose met them at the gate to Stony Man Farm. Her blond hair flashed in the morning light.

"Don't go to your quarters, don't bother with anything," she said. "I've put your overnight bags and equipment cases on the helicopter. Here's your mission authorization from Mack—" she passed a tight roll of teletype paper to Blancanales.

"Where are we going?" Lyons asked.

"California. And I tell you, this one's worse than New York. Good luck."

April watched them as they sprinted the last hundred yards across a landing field to the waiting Huey. The chopper's idling rotor blades accelerated to a shriek. The skids left the ground as Lyons and Blancanales leapt in the side door. Gadgets Schwarz, already strapped in, glanced up, grinned in greeting, went back to reading a teletype printout; he wore only a bathrobe and pajama bottoms.

Hal Brognola was unshaved and his hair uncombed. He gave the three members of Able Team their intercom headsets. "Close those side doors, the briefing starts now." Brognola spoke into his headset's microphone. "Pilots, take off your headphones. Don't put them on until we approach the airport.

"Half an hour ago," Brognola began, "two-thirty California time, a motorcycle gang called 'The Outlaws' seized Santa Catalina Island."

"The Outlaws did what?" gasped Lyons.

"Let me continue. There are about seventy, seventy-five of them and as of now they are in control of the island. They have severed all communications to the mainland. They have killed or captured all the law-enforcement officers. Somehow, they took every resident of Avalon hostage. That's about fourteen hundred people, we aren't sure exactly how many. Avalon is a tourist town—there may be as many as a hundred tourists who are spending the weekend there."

Hal Brognola was Able Team's commanding officer, a burly older man answerable by choice to Mack Bolan (a.k.a. Col. John Phoenix) and by duty to the White House. He paused to ensure that his grim news was fully understood by the three men before him.

"The leader of the Outlaws, someone with the name of 'Horse,' called the Governor of California direct, on the Governor's secret hot line. That, in itself, is a significant point. That hot line number is classified. It is known only to the Governor's aides and a few military officials."

Brognola paused to refer to a printout.

"The gang leader made these demands. The release of three of their members now in prison. Twenty million dollars in gold. And a nuclear submarine to deliver the three gang members and the gold. The assumption is that Horse will then force the submarine's crew at gunpoint to transport the gang to some foreign country."

"Has any of this crazy stuff actually been confirmed?" asked the benign Blancanales. "Isn't there any chance it could all be—"

"No chance. It is confirmed. Though *officially* we're saying it's a prank. A Deputy Sheriff managed to make a shortwave Mayday call. The ships that reported the message have been told it was a loony tune.

"But when a Coast Guard helicopter flew over the town, it was fired on by light and heavy caliber machine guns." Hal sighed.

"The gang leader has threatened to kill ten hostages the next time any ship or aircraft approaches the island. His people control the port's radar station. Anything comes within three miles, he kills ten people.

"He has given the Governor forty-eight hours to deliver the ransom."

Lyons spoke. "How many people have they killed?"

"That's not known. However, he had a captured Deputy Sheriff—apparently the same officer who put out the Mayday—speak to the Governor. As the Governor listened, he heard the officer begin a prayer, then there was a shot."

Lyons closed his eyes for a moment. "That's the Outlaws. That's the way they work. Murder and mutilation," he murmured. "Once, when they were moving in on the East L.A. drug trade, they captured one of our undercover officers. They sent his skin to us in a box. With a cassette tape. They had skinned him alive and recorded the entire procedure.

"And we never got them for that. You know how it is, a case has to be textbook perfect to prosecute."

"The Outlaws' constitutional rights," Brognola commanded, "are hereby suspended—"

"Kayaks!" Gadgets blurted. "We'll take a boat as close as the three-mile limit, then paddle in. Fiberglass or canvas kayaks, with fiberglass paddles, a few inches of plastic foam over the equipment. There won't be any radar bounce off of plastic. And besides, a kayak rides only a few inches above the water. The equipment will actually be below the waterline.

"I was thinking of wind-surfing, but there might not be any wind, so...."

Gadgets' enthusiasm made Lyons grin. He glanced to the others, pointed at Schwarz. "You know, this guy is a wizard. Sometimes I wonder why he isn't a millionaire."

"Government work doesn't pay that good," said Gadgets. "But the benefits are okay. Travel, education, meeting interesting people, a good pension—"

Chances were they'd never collect a pension. Blancanales changed the subject.

"What about the media?"

"It is impossible to keep the press from investigating," Brognola said. "The first reporter who tries to check out the prank story will know something is wrong. We will need to cancel the tourist boat that shuttles back and forth between Los Angeles Harbor and the island. And the Coast Guard will be preventing any private craft from approaching the island. The most we can hope for is a few hours before the questions start. After that...." Brognola shrugged.

"And what happens if we *can't* break them?" Blancanales continued.

"Ask the Governor."

"That's not going to happen!" Lyons shouted. "I

owe those scum from way back. As far as I'm concerned, this is do or die.''

Gravity shifted as the helicopter banked. Blue sky filled one side door window. Blancanales glanced down at the concrete runway and parked Air Force jets, to the jet waiting for them. He turned back to Lyons.

"They don't call us unless it's do or die.''

Still wearing sweatsuits, Lyons and Blancanales carried their bags into the forward cabin of the Air Force jet that would take them to Los Angeles. A man waited for them at the conference table. Behind him was a stack of aluminum cases in anodized black.

Wide-shouldered, thick-necked, with huge forearms and large hands, his hair clipped to a stubble, this man looked like a Marine Corps drill instructor.

But when he stood to greet them, he first pushed himself up with his arms, then used two forearm-clamp crutches to rise to his full height. His knees locked straight with metallic snaps.

"Andrzej Konzaki," he introduced himself, extending his hand, his right crutch hanging by the forearm clamp.

"Pleased to meet you." Blancanales shook hands with him.

Lyons didn't. "Who are you?"

"You mean, why am I here?" Konzaki smiled. "Is that not correct, Mr. Lyons?"

"Andrzej has clearance," Brognola called. He was struggling up the aisle with one of Gadgets' cases. Gadgets followed with a second case.

Engines shrieked. The jet taxied to take-off position on the runway. Lyons and Gadgets shook hands with Konzaki. They all took seats around the conference table, and strapped themselves in.

"Though we haven't met before," Konzaki told them, "we have worked together. You, Mr. Lyons, spoke with me only a few weeks ago, concerning some very unusual ammunition for a very difficult situation. I am Special Weapons Development, CIA. I viewed the video tapes, and I attended the autopsies of those Puerto Rican terrorists. Did you not think the results remarkable?"

"Yeah. Remarkable."

"And not one of the hostages," Konzaki continued, "suffered wounds from bullets or bullet fragments."

Konzaki eased back into his chair. He opened his attaché case. "Before I present the tools for your present mission, let me continue with the briefing, courtesy of some data put together by your Mr. Brognola.

"Here are maps of Santa Catalina Island. Satellite photos. Los Angeles Police Department files on the Outlaws motorcycle gang for the last fifteen years."

The last folder Konzaki distributed to each of the members of Able Team contained a three-inch thick stack of photocopied forms and typewritten pages. Gadgets flipped through the stack he received:

"With this much attention, you'd think the LAPD would have known about the attack on Catalina."

"Don't knock the LAPD," Lyons spoke up, sensitive about his former job. "Five thousand cops for a city of almost four million people. You figure it out."

Brognola flipped through the folder, found a particular section. "Actually, the police were onto it. They have details on the theft of military weapons, the warehousing of civilian weapons and ammunition, and the assembly of all the California Outlaws in the Los Angeles area. They knew *something* was about to happen."

Konzaki swiveled his chair at that point and opened one of the several cases stacked behind him. He placed a scoped, bolt-action rifle on the conference table.

"This is a Mannlicher SSG in .308 NATO," he announced. "You're familiar with the Starlite scope. You'll notice I have fabricated a mount for the Starlite which will allow the use of the iron sights during the day.

"Here are a hundred 'Accelerator' rounds. With a velocity of over 4000 feet per second, the 'Accelerators' will make long-distance snap shots possible.

"Here are ten rounds like those you used in the New York tower hijacking. They will kill without creating a through-and-through wound. And, as you remember, a head shot is utterly devastating.

"Here are ten rounds with Teflon-coated steel slugs. They will punch through any vehicle. Almost any wall.

"Here are ten tracers. You might use them as incendiary rounds. I have a hundred rounds of hollow points, if you want them. However, this is not a fire fight weapon. Also, the police file reveals that these criminals have stolen considerable numbers of assault rifles chambered in .308 NATO. Rather than carry additional and perhaps unnecessary ammunition, I say capture the stuff."

He opened another case and brought out an odd-looking pistol with a short suppressor mounted on the barrel. "This is a Beretta Model 93R modified for silence. I have attached the suppressor and changed the springs to cycle sub-sonic 9mm cartridges. It fires single shots or three round bursts—"

"What's the cyclic rate?" Gadgets asked, intrigued.

"Practical rate of fire, approximately 110 rounds per minute. This lever folds down for the left hand and the left thumb slips through the extra large trigger guard. With both hands, short range burst accuracy is excellent.

"Here's a holster and gun belt. The pouches have fifteen magazines, each containing fifteen sub-sonic cartridges.

"In case you expend all that ammunition, this pouch contains the pistol's standard springs. I'll show you how to disassemble the pistol and replace the springs. That will allow the use of full velocity ammunition, though it will no longer be silent."

He opened another case. "Here are some standard weapons, with minor modifications. An Ingram in 9mm. And an Uzi. Both throated to feed hollowpoints. I have also added flash hiders. Magazines and ammunition for both.

"Here are some small LAAW rockets, one for armor or barricade penetration, two with antipersonnel warheads.

"I also have this box of grenades for you, fragmentation and white phosphorous. And for Mr. Schwarz, radio-triggered detonators in several frequencies."

Lyons grinned. "All right! Christmas comes early. The odds just took a turn in our favor. But tell me—"

A buzzer interrupted him. Brognola went to the door separating the passenger area from the pilot's cabin, unlocked and opened it. A flight officer spoke quietly with him, then handed him a sheet of notes.

"This complicates it," Brognola said, returning to the group. "The Pentagon have six of their theoreticians on the island. Boffins, unarmed. Specialists in lasers, particle beams and atomic fields. You have got to bring those men out, no matter what. Highest national security priority. When we get to L.A., we'll have photos and dossiers waiting for you."

"What are they doing there?" Gadgets asked.

"It says they wanted a quiet place for intensive talks."

"Ha!" Lyons laughed bitterly. He turned to Konzaki. "What I want to know—did you put all this together in an hour? Are you a magician?"

"No." Konzaki spoke with infinite sadness. "I assembled several groups of weapons, each group suitable for different locales in the world, and different circumstances. I am not a magician, nor can I foretell the future, Mr. Lyons. I simply read the newspaper. I knew it would only be a matter of time before these weapons were needed."

5

Chris Davis lay in the dark, listening to Mrs. Shepard comfort her husband. Mr. Shepard, though battered and bleeding, sometimes doubling over with pain in his gut, had been silent until he slipped into sleep. Then he moaned and cried out. His wife held his head, smoothed his hair, pulled blankets around him.

He startled awake, and stared into the darkness around him. "It's okay," his wife whispered. "We're all right, it was only a nightmare—"

"You mean what I dreamed?" he asked her. "Or what's happening? Kid," he called, and Chris jumped up, "get me a bucket or something so I don't mess up your dad's study."

Mr. Shepard had suggested to the boys that they all sleep in the one room. As the den opened to the patio, their voices or flashlights would not betray them to Outlaws patrolling the street. If the Outlaws fired into the house, then two walls and Mr. Davis' shelves of law books protected them.

And they could watch and listen for movement in the backyard while one of them stood guard in the front room. Chris took a towel and a bowl to Mrs. Shepard, then joined Roger and their friend Jack in the front room.

He saw Jack smoking a joint. "Man! This ain't no party. You could get killed."

"Hey, man," Jack laughed. "This is the best party yet. We're going to kill some bikers. They show up, they die! Bang, bang."

"I told him," Roger said, shaking his head.

"Yeah, well I'm telling him again. Listen to this, jerk. If the bikers out there see that joint or your lighter, they're going to know someone's in here."

"Yeah. Well, okay. I'm going to catch some sleep. Wake me up when you see some targets." He blew smoke at them and returned to the den.

"They don't call him Jack-off for nothing," whispered Chris.

"I wish you hadn't given him that gun," said Roger.

"He's a jerk but he is on our side. We need all the help we can get. I think Mr. Shepard's going to die."

"I thought he only got punched out."

"Nah, he's all broken up inside. He's trying to be cool in front of his wife, but I think he's puking blood. If he can't get to a hospital, he could bleed to death in his guts—"

"Up there! Bikers! At the end of the street." Roger pointed up the block, to where their street ended in a three-way intersection with a cross street.

The bikers went into the house. Chris and Roger watched the lights go on. Shadows crowded one window, the window opened. From it could be seen the entire length of their street.

After the bikers left the house, the lights went out. One of the them pushed a motorcycle deep into the driveway, where it could not be seen from the street. Then the bikers left.

"One of them's stayed in that house," Roger said. "Watching the street."

"I'll get Mr. Shepard." Chris went into the study, and returned with the shaky adult.

"How you feeling, Mr. Shepard?" Roger asked.

"Fantastic." His face was too swollen for a grin. "So what's the problem?"

"That house over there," Roger pointed. "The Outlaws left a man in it to watch the street. They've got us trapped."

"You said you had it worse than this, Mr. Shepard. Were you in Vietnam?" Chris asked.

"I did all my fighting on Wilshire Boulevard and in front of the Pentagon in Washington. The name's Glen—"

"Your wife said you were in the army."

"They drafted me. It was prison or the Airborne. My mom and dad talked me into going, said Vietnam was all over, why not do my duty? Well, I went through basic, advanced infantry training, special weapons school, then they sent me to school to learn Laotian. That was in 1972, and they're teaching me to speak the Laos languages?"

Glen warmed to his story. His wounds had put him in the right mood for it.

"I told the Commandant of Fort Ord that if he tried to ship me out without declaring war, it would be my duty to resist. And the first criminal I'd shoot would be him.

"That was a quick ticket to the stockade, but I didn't go to Laos. They figured I was crazy so I did eighteen months in the psychiatric ward. Drugs, electro-shock, beatings—''

"Huh," Chris puzzled. "So that's why you're so political."

"This man knows the truth. Now let's figure out how to snuff that sniper."

"You can't do anything, Mr. Shepard. You're hurt."

"You want to do it?" Glen Shepard asked bluntly. "Think you can kill a man in cold blood?" The boys didn't answer. "I was trained to defend my country. Right now, my wife and you and the neighborhood people are my country."

Leaning his M-14 rifle against the window ledge, Acidhead dropped a pinch of PCP onto a rolling paper, added some Mexican marijuana, and rolled up. He leaned back into the easy chair and touched a flame to the joint. "Dusted!" he laughed, watching the street through heavily lidded eyes.

Headlights and taillights streaked across the far end of the street; the rumble of motorcycle engines came loud, then faded. A patrol, thought Acidhead. He stared at the trees overhanging the quiet street. Dawn-gray sky showed through the canopy of branches. He took a few more hits of the cheap dust and cheaper marijuana. The pattern of dark branches and graying sky suddenly reversed, the sky a mass of jagged fragments exploding from darkness all of a sudden.

He shook his head to clear his vision. "Can't get too far out there," he mumbled to himself. He ground out the half-smoked joint. "Gotta do some killing."

A wiry man, Acidhead stood less than six feet even in his thick-soled riding boots. He wore his curly hair and beard cut to the same two inch length; hair stuck out straight from his head, giving him a surprised look at all times. His bulging eyes added to the impression.

"Acidhead, this is Horse," the hand radio squawked from the window ledge. "You in position?"

"Wherever I am, I'm here and ready."

"You got much fog there?"

"I can see a block or so."

"You know what to do. Anything that don't wear our colors, kill it."

Watching for movement on the street, Acidhead thought of the people who lived there. Upstanding citizens. Righteous, God-fearing people. Daddy, mommy, the little kiddies. When he cruised the freeways on his bike, they were the people who stared at him like he was some kind of human-shaped shit.

He'd get his chance. All the guys guarding the crowd in the Casino talked about how many teeny-boppers they'd rape. Forget the teeny-boppers, Acidhead thought. When he pulled guard duty, he'd take the real young ones.

Fantasizing, he picked up the half-smoked joint, relit it. He thought of how they'd cry and scream. What would the good people think of that?

Easing himself over the last fence, Glen Shepard dropped to the sidewalk and stayed crouched in a shadow cast by a streetlight. He unslung the short-barreled shotgun, watching the street for bikers.

Wearing his dark slacks, and a black leather jacket and black stocking cap borrowed from the Davis boys, he hoped he looked like an Outlaw. He moved from shadow to shadow until he saw the sniper's window. A lighter flared, the biker's face emerged from the darkness, then was gone as the flame died. But the red point of a cigarette glowed. Glen watched the window for a minute. He saw only the one cigarette, heard no voices.

Calculating the angles, Glen saw how he could cross over the street. The trunk of a large tree on the opposite side blocked a part of the sniper's field of fire. If Glen stayed within that narrow area, he could cross unobserved.

But he was visible from everywhere else. He would have to take his chances. Soon it would be daylight. Then the Outlaws would sweep the neighborhood, searching every house, flushing out the residents.

Crawling to stay beneath the screen of a low hedge, he watched the window. When it disappeared behind the tree trunk, he stood up, stepped over the hedge, walked. He couldn't run. The pain in his gut flared with every step. If he ran, he'd puke again.

Expecting a bullet, he forced himself to swagger, holding the shotgun loosely in one hand. At the far curb, he strolled into the tree's shadow, then dropped flat, and crawled into the driveway of the house. He painfully snaked up the porch steps, praying there was nothing in the darkness to knock over.

A voice broke the stillness. He cringed, pointing the shotgun. It was the hand-radio, holding forth from the window only six feet from him.

"Acidhead! Come in, you there? Wake up!"

"Yeah, I'm awake. What?"

"This is Charlie. You kill anything yet?"

"Nothing to shoot at...."

"You will have in half an hour. Happy hunting, over."

As he listened, Glen slid the last few feet to the window. A window screen leaned against the house. He saw the forestock and barrel of a military rifle sticking out a foot from the window.

So slowly that his thighs shook from the strain, Glen stood up. He shifted the shotgun from his right hand to his left, slipped the Davis family's twelve-inch stainless steel carving knife from his belt. He held it low.

"Hey, Acidhead," Glen Shepard hissed. "You got a smoke?"

"Who's there?"

"The bogeyman. You got a smoke, I'm all out of the good stuff."

Leaning from the window, the biker looked in both directions, saw Glen. "You gotta be careful, I coulda shot—"

Thrusting upward, Glen jammed the long blade through the biker's throat and up into his brain, pushing through cartilage and bone. The dead man convulsed, snapping the blade off inside his skull. Glen was left with only the handle and four inches of blade.

"Hey, Acidhead, you okay?" Glen asked, speaking loud, testing the environment. "What's with you? Anybody else here? Help me with him, will you?"

But no one answered. Shotgun ahead of him, Glen

stepped through the window. In seconds, he stripped the dead man of his Outlaw jacket, his weapons, and the walkie-talkie.

Electric stars sparkled overhead in the domed ceiling of the Avalon Casino Ballroom. Beneath the false heavens, the imprisoned people of Catalina—men, women and children: residents and tourists—waited, agonized. Some tried to sleep on the dance floor. Most sprawled on the floor or paced through the crowd. Numbed and silenced by fear, many stared into space, ignoring the other prisoners around them.

Max Stevens refused to surrender to his fears. Leaving his wife and teenage daughter with a group of friends, he limped through the crowd. He saw crying men, sobbing women, men and women with faces twisted by barely restrained hysteria. Despite the ballroom's humid warmth, he still wore his coat. He searched through the crowd, found men and women who were still calm and thinking. He quizzed each hostage as he spotted them:

"You want to talk about getting out of here?" he asked a young woman.

"How? What are you going to do?"

"I don't know yet, but if we get the chance, we should be ready."

"I'm willing to listen—"

"Not just listen. I want to hear your ideas." Then he moved on to the next person.

"You think we can break out?" he asked a bath-robed man.

"Maybe. Those creeps aren't supermen."

"Tell me when I get back with the others." Max

pressed on, always searching for the faces of the acquaintances he trusted.

"Max Stevens! You okay?" One of the island's resident fishermen held him by the shoulders. "I saw them shoving you around."

"I tried to get away."

"That's my man!" The fisherman leaned close. "Think a knife could help us get out of here?" He pulled up his pants leg, revealing a knife handle in his boot.

Max grinned. "They didn't search me, either. Think fourteen rounds of .45 caliber hollow point might open some doors for us? I got my Hardballer and two magazines."

The fisherman's face crinkled into a wide grin. "Might help."

"Don't go anywhere," Max told him. "I'm looking for more recruits."

He found many, but searched for more, crisscrossing the ballroom, looking into the faces of everyone there. Screams and shouts stopped his search. He joined a crowd gathering around a scuffle.

Two Outlaws were beating and kicking a middle-aged man as two others dragged away a pretty teenage girl. A woman lay gasping on the floor, doubled-over, her face bleeding from several blows.

"What's happening there?" Max asked an onlooker.

"Those animals saw a girl they wanted. The girl's mother and father tried to stop them. I wish I hadn't left my gun in the house."

"You want to do something about it?"

"No! Max, no!" His wife Carol had come to the crowd. She jerked him back. Pressing close to him, she clutched at the weapon under his coat. "If you try anything, even if you kill them, kill ten of them, you'll die. You've got Julia and me to think of. No matter what, you'll be killed. They've got machine guns for God's sake!"

Max looked helplessly at the Outlaws. They dragged the shrieking, pleading teenager out of the ballroom. His wife took his face in her hands, made him look at her. "She'll probably live, Max. Don't throw your life away. Someday, she'll forget. If they kill you, I'll never forget."

He listened to his wife, his lips a bloodless line across his face. He looked over at the beaten man and woman. As the bikers walked away, a few onlookers went to the aid of the bloodied couple, covering them with coats, wiping the broken teeth and blood from the man's mouth. Max looked back to his wife:

"What if the next girl they want is Julia?"

6

Luck blessed Able Team with fog.

Maintaining a distance of four miles off the western coast of Santa Catalina Island, the Coast Guard cutter lowered a steel boarding ramp to within a few inches of the water, then launched the three kayaks at intervals of a half mile. After the cutter faded into the fog, its wake and propeller foam dissipated and the surface of the sea returned to a mirror calm.

They floated in a gray void unbroken by sound or daylight, the only motion a gentle groundswell bobbing the fiberglass kayaks.

"Well, all right!" Lyons called out, his voice lost in the emptiness. "This is fun!" He tried the double-bladed paddle, going straight for a few strokes, then spun the kayak in a circle as he watched the wobbling needle of the compass that was epoxied to the deck of the kayak.

"I'd be nowhere without this compass," he said out loud. "In fact I *am* nowhere...."

A splash broke the water. Lyons whipped his head around to see a shadow and a fin move under the ocean's surface. He remembered the recent news accounts of Great White sharks attacking surfers. Search teams had recovered only body parts and pieces of shark-gnawed surfboards. He touched the butt of the Colt Python shoulder-holstered under his black rain slicker, then paddled furiously to the west. "Hope it was a seal," he chanted. "Hope it was a porpoise, hope it was a dolphin. . . ."

Less than an hour after the cutter had cast him into the Pacific, Gadgets spotted the rocky shore. Though the fog still held, from time to time sunlight flashed on the water. Wind came and went, allowing him glimpses of sage-covered hillsides. In a few minutes, he knew, he would be visible from shore.

Off to the south, his right, he saw a wave rise to a wall, then arc over. The curl created a tunnel of churning foam, then the wave collapsed, shooting spray. Gadgets angled toward the pattern of white water that the wave had left. If he could get the force of the white water behind him, he would surf the last two hundred yards.

He paddled hard for a minute. He seemed no closer than before to the peaking waves. Maybe it was a current, he thought, as he kept on paddling.

Glancing behind him, he suddenly understood. He had misjudged the distance. He had thought the waves small, and only a few hundred feet away. No, they were several times that distance, and over ten feet in height, like the wave walling behind him.

Thinking first of the electronics inside the kayak, Gadgets checked the plastic and elastic seal closing the gap between the hole in the kayak's deck and his body. It was tight. He gave his black plastic rain slicker a quick tuck into the elastic seal, then stroked hard and fast with the paddles, spray flying behind him. His only hope was to be ahead of the wave when the top came down.

Feeling the wave lift him, he knew he'd lost the race. The kayak stood vertical on the wave face for an instant, then, as the wave curled over him, blocking out the sky, at the moment he expected to be thrown into the churning vortex, the kayak slipped down the wave, accelerating.

He hurtled through darkness and the roar of the wave around him overwhelmed his thoughts, and for a moment his fear too. Instinctively, he leaned toward the light beyond the curl. The roar became so loud he seemed to be flying through silence.

Light circled by a vast, spinning vortex rushed toward him, and then he burst out. Salvation. But above him still, the wave's face towered, a wall of water defying gravity and overhanging him.

Keeping the paddle out of the water that blurred beneath him, Gadgets leaned forward until his arms and chest rested on the deck of the kayak. Whether from reduced wind resistance or improved hydrodynamics or both, he gained speed, leaving the roaring curl behind him. Soon he skipped far ahead of the critical section and into almost flat water. Still moving fast, he sat up and looked for shore.

Rocks! A previous wave's backwash rolled toward him, the kayak bouncing, then the wave behind him leaped up and crashed, and the white water engulfed him. He dug in with the paddle, trying to slow his rush onto the rocks.

Fiberglass shrieked. He felt several quick lurches, then the foam drove him onto a pebbled beach. As the backwash tried to tug him back, he jammed the paddle into the pebbles and jumped from the kayak. He quickly pulled the craft above the waterline.

He sat on a rock shaking, trying to calm his heartbeat. He took long, slow breaths. He could not re-member being so scared in a long, long while.

He noticed some small rocks in a circle, scorched by campfire, and a discarded sandal, and some beer cans. Spray-painted across one large rock were the words: "Surfers Rule."

Here he was shaking, and teenagers did it for thrills.

Gadgets went to work. He glanced every few sec-onds to the hillsides above him as he stripped the plastic bag from his Uzi, snapped in a magazine, and chambered a round.

He examined the kayak and realized it would not float again. Long rips had broken open the fiberglass bottom. Near the nose, a snapped flap of fiberglass exposed the plywood frame. He unloaded his equip-ment and other weapons and pushed the kayak back into the water. The wash pulled it out to the shore break, and the first wave sank it.

He assembled his electronics. First, the scanner/auto-recorder. The LAPD file on the Outlaws had noted the theft of a case of high-quality walkie-talkies. If the Outlaws were using those radios, Gadgets' scanner could monitor and record the con-versation automatically.

Then he extended the antenna of his hand-radio and keyed a click-code. Two beeps for onshore and safe, three beeps to identify himself. His scanner/auto-recorder picked up the beeps, recorded the signal on the cassette.

Voices came on. "This is Chief, this is Chief." "Horse here. What?" "We cleaned up Little Har-bor. Had to kill a Park Ranger. We're sending back a couple of families we found at the campground. Couple of good-looking women in the crowd. We took turns on one, saved the other one for you if you're interested." "Don't waste your time on that, you're on patrol." "Sorry, it just sorta happened." "You watching the ocean? Any ships, boats?" "Use the radar. There's too much fog here." "Okay, but keep patrolling the beaches the best you can. Over and out."

Gadgets hurried through the assembly of the rest of his equipment: the long-range directional microphone, the radio-triggered detonators. After what he had heard, he understood that every minute of delay meant death and degradation for the people of the island. As he shouldered his backpack, another voice came from the scanner, on a different frequency: "Horse, this is your friend. Answer." "Yes, sir! This is Horse. Is there anything you need?" "No, everything's fine. I'm quite comfortable. Brief me. Is the seizure of the island complete?" "Oh, yeah. No problems. Some shooting. Had to kill some heroes." "What about the conversations with the Governor?" "Nothing else with the Governor. They said they'd be sending the submarine. They put a negotiator on the line, but I just hung up." "Good. Follow the plan. Soon we will be very wealthy men." "Yessir! That's what I want." Then there was static.

Who was that man? He called himself a "friend" of these biker sadists? The man with the calm, educated voice was a co-conspirator with Horse. Who was he?

Gadgets' thoughts were interrupted by clicks on the radio. Two clicks, then two more. Blancanales.

Another set of clicks answered. Two clicks, then one. Lyons. Gadgets keyed his hand-radio as he went up the hillside toward the rendezvous.

On shore and ready, Able Team were moving into action.

Striding through the sagebrush, Blancanales listened for voices or motorcycles. He had heard large-caliber rifle fire only seconds after reaching shore, but Lyons' and Gadgets' click-code replies calmed his fears. The rifle fire had not been aimed at them. Now his concern was to avoid it being aimed at him.

He glanced at his compass and the plastic-covered topographical map, then surveyed what terrain he could see for landmarks. Light fog still shrouded the hillsides. Continuing due south, he followed a cattle trail through the low brush, inspecting it for foot or tire tracks.

Below him he heard surf. Then when a canyon's breeze carried away the fog for a moment, he saw the rocky shoreline. Above him the sun rose from behind the unseen peaks; it became a gray disk. Soon the sun would burn away the fog. He hurried his pace, counting cadence to himself.

Footprints appeared on the cow trail. Blancanales stopped for a second to check the tracks. Jogging shoes, yesterday, maybe the day before. Cow hooves had crossed the shoe tracks. There was a dry cow-paddy over one of the prints. Going on, he saw more and more footprints—jogging shoes, hiking boots, sandals, even a high-heel shoe—and some cow tracks. Bubble gum wrappers, cigarette butts and drink cans indicated frequent visitors.

He checked the map again. He knew the Little Harbor campground was only a few hundred yards farther. He cut due east, staying in the narrow creek bed of a small canyon. The tangled brush and loose rocks slowed him to a hand-over-hand climb, but the steep sides of the gully and the overhanging branches protected him from being observed.

A retaining wall of sheer concrete blocked his progress. He saw the guardrail of a road above him. Not wanting to chance the road, he paralleled it, staying close to the hillside as he followed animal and foot trails.

At first, he thought the sounds were gull-cries from the ocean. He listened harder. It was laughter, coarse laughter, coming from the campground.

Unsnapping the flap of his Browning Double-Action's holster, he slipped out the pistol. Then he changed his mind. Always use the proper technology, Konzaki had said. Blancanales found the Beretta 93R in his backpack, slapped in a magazine and snapped back the slide.

He hid the backpack. Soft-footing it along the trail, crouching below the level of the brush, he could hear screams, more laughter, voices. He continued another hundred yards and came to some sort of fire road. He couldn't go any farther without losing cover. But another scream told him he was was already there.

Fifty yards below, two Outlaws raped a woman. One struggled on top of the naked, shrieking woman. The other biker stood on her arms, looking down at her and the biker and laughing, urging the biker on, taunting him.

The standing biker also taunted the woman's husband. The man lay against a car, bound hand and foot. He was turning his head away. Inside the car, a child cried.

Blancanales surveyed the scene. The fire road cut straight down the steep hillside, ending at the gravel and asphalt of the campground. The Outlaws and the unfortunate family were at the bottom of the fire road.

He saw only two motorcycles at this particular campsite. He looked beyond to the other campsites. He saw collapsed tents, scattered belongings, but no other motorcycles.

Sliding and crawling as fast as he dared through the thick sagebrush, Blancanales silently closed the distance between himself and the bikers. Twenty yards uphill from the campsite, he could not risk getting closer.

Prone in the brush, only his hands extending from cover, he grasped the Beretta in both hands, right hand on the grip, left hand holding the extension lever in front of the trigger guard, his left thumb through the extra-large trigger guard as Konzaki had demonstrated. He sighted on the standing biker's chest, gave him a three-round burst.

The bullets interrupted a laugh, the first round punching into his chest, the second his collar-bone, the third taking away his left eye and sideburn. He fell backward and thrashed on the gravel.

There had been no sound other than the slap of the almost simultaneous impacts. The other Outlaw looked up from the woman, puzzled by his friend's fall. Blancanales flicked down the selector to single shot. He sighted on the biker's head.

The woman clawed the biker in the face, and twisted out from under him. She blocked Blancanales' aim. He broke cover, ran and slid and jumped down the hillside. The biker scrambled to his feet, his pants around his knees, trying to pull a pistol from a shoulder holster.

The snap shot glanced off the top of the biker's head, sent him staggering backwards. Blancanales finally reached the bottom of the hill, dropped into a two-handed, wide-leg stance to deliver the kill shot, when the woman again blocked his aim as she kicked and punched the bleeding biker.

"Get down!" Blancanales shouted. "Out of the way! Let me kill him!"

She turned and saw him for the first time. Her eyes went wide at the sight of the black-clad warrior with the pistol. But she didn't move. The biker sprinted away, weaving through trees and brush. Blancanales sighted, fired again, heard the bullet slap the biker. He fell, scrambled up, kept running.

Starting after the wounded biker, Blancanales yelled back at the woman:

"Take that dead man's weapons, you all go hide in the brush somewhere. Don't show yourself till you see uniformed police officers or soldiers. Move it—I can't help you any more!"

"Thank you, oh, thank you, thank you. God be with you," the woman sobbed as he ran.

He followed the blood trail through the campground. Ahead of him was a cluster of park buildings surrounded by bushes and trees. The blood led in that direction. Off to his left, the camp road curved through brush and trees shading the camping sites.

Not to risk walking into the wounded man's ambush, Blancanales took the road, He would circle around, kill him.

He jogged past the park buildings, then spotted a trail through the campsites and trees that led back to the buildings. If the biker was waiting for him, that trail would allow Blancanales to surprise him. He left the road and pressed through thick branches. He held the Beretta ready in front of him.

A rifle butt slammed into the back of his head. He fell hard, didn't move. A biker stood over him. He was pointing a Heckler and Koch G-3 assault rifle at the motionless Blancanales.

"Well, well, well. What is this?"

Waiting at the rendezvous point, Lyons and Gadgets repeatedly sent out the click-code for the third member of Able Team. They received no answer until the scanner/auto-recorder spoke:

"Well, Horse. This here is Rebel out at the Little Harbor camping ground. Guess what? We got ourselves a commando." "What? He alive?" "Yeah, for a while. We were thinking of—" "I want him! Bring him here!" "All we got is bikes, man. He could get away." "I'll send a car. You don't touch him, unnerstan'? He's mine!"

Lyons and Gadgets didn't wait to hear every word. Sprinting through the brush, they already knew the sadist's message:

Horrible death for Pol Blancanales.

7

Finally coming to the hillcrest, Lyons stumbled the last few steps, then had to fall, coughing. On his hands and knees he spat long ropes of mucus into the dirt. He had attempted to sprint up the hill with a fifty-pound backpack of weapons and equipment. Though his sprinting steps had slowed to a determined march, he had not stopped. His friend's life depended on him.

Glancing back, Lyons saw Gadgets still struggling up the slope. Packing more weight—weapons, electronics, and heavy nickle-cadmium batteries—and lacking Lyons' fanatical physical conditioning, Gadgets straggled a hundred yards behind him. Lyons slipped out of his backpack straps, snapped open the "Daylight" Mannlicher's fiberglass and foam case, and crawled to the ridgeline.

Though the morning remained gray and cool, the light breeze had blown away the fog. The scope's eight-power optics closed the distance between Lyons and the campground a couple of hundred yards below. He saw three bikers standing in front of Blancanales. With heavy wire twisted around his wrists, Blancanales hung by his hands from a utility pole, his boots swinging a few inches from the asphalt of the parking lot.

A biker with a bloody head waved a knife. As Lyons watched, the biker touched the blade tip to Blancanales' eye. Lyons whipped back the Mannlicher's bolt, chambered a .308 Accelerator. But one of the other Outlaws, a lanky, slow-moving biker wearing a Confederate army cap, shoved the bloodied biker away from the prisoner. The third biker popped open a beer can and swilled the drink.

Setting the rifle's safety, Lyons glanced to the gravel and dirt road leading across the island to Avalon. He saw no one.

Gadgets collapsed beside Lyons. His throat rasped with every breath. As he choked down the coughs, he pulled a pair of binoculars from a side pocket of his pack and focused on the scene below.

"Only those three? See any others?"

"Not yet," murmured Lyons. "You want to stay here? Work the rifle?"

"You're going down there?"

"Over there—" Lyons pointed north, to the road continuing past the campgrounds. A hundred yards from where the bikers held Blancanales, the road curved behind a hillside. "—I'll drop down on the far side of that hill and come back through the campsites. Trees and bushes all the way. Lots of cover."

Gadgets looked at his watch. "We intercepted the message eight minutes ago. Assuming they left one minute later and are now driving at thirty miles an hour over the mountain, we've got nineteen minutes until they get here."

"And what if they drive sixty?" Lyons gave Gadgets the Mannlicher. "The safety's on. There's a fast one in the chamber. If you see them coming on the road, kill those three down there, open up on the car.

I'm taking your Uzi. You hear me open up, kill those three and watch for targets. See you later.''

Lyons buckled the bandolier of thirty-round magazines around his chest, then snatched up the Uzi. Sliding and running down the hillside, he paralleled the ridgeline for a hundred and fifty yards, finally angling upward to the crest. He crawled over the concrete-hard dirt of a firebreak, and looked to the south as he went over the top. Hillsides and trees blocked the bikers' view of him. He took the time to scan the road and campground hundreds of yards below him.

There was no movement. He listened for motorcycle engines, heard only the squawks of sea gulls picking over garbage in the campground.

He started down the steep firebreak. His feet slipped on dirt and loose gravel. Instead of digging his heels in, he let gravity take him, skiing down the firebreak on his boot soles. When the slope leveled for a few yards, Lyons ran, then jumped into space, flexing his knees as he hit. He dirt-skied again to the road, and crossed it without slowing.

Instead of continuing down the firebreak without cover, he plunged into the brush, running in a crouch. He held the Uzi at arm's length, using the small weapon to part branches.

Shots! He fell flat. He heard laughter and voices. Silently, he crawled through the sagebrush. He slithered into a gully not much wider than his shoulders. He followed the gully until he came to a grating of welded reinforcing rods. Beyond the grate, a concrete spillway dropped down a vertical embankment to the parking lot.

At the far end of the parking lot, two bikers

taunted Pol Blancanales. The third, the biker wearing the Confederate army cap, braced his G-3 assault rifle on his motorcycle and fired at the gulls that soared in the gray sky.

Lyons took the hand-radio from the thigh-pocket of his black battle suit. He checked the volume and called Gadgets.

"Wizard, what you see?"

"I saw you. Where are you now?"

"Maybe a hundred feet to the north of them. We've got to do this all at once, I can't rush them from here. I've got a good angle on the two in front of Pol. Think you can hit Johnny Reb without putting a hole through the motorcycle?"

"Negative. Unless— He's standing up. Want to do it right now?"

Lyons rested the Uzi on the re-bar gate, sighted through the peep sight on the biker with the knife. "Waiting for you."

Watching through the peep sight, Lyons saw the bloodied Outlaw whip his head around as the roar-shriek of the ultrahigh-velocity slug ripped apart the quiet morning. Lyons fired the split second he heard the big rifle's report.

Blood spurted from the biker's chest. The single 9mm slug had punched through his heart. Lyons found the other man, tightened his aim, calmly squeezed off a single shot as the biker spun around, his head whipping back and forth as he searched the hillsides for the attackers. The shot caught him in the arm and ribs, knocking him down. He tried to crawl, but his broken arm collapsed underneath him.

Should we take him for interrogation? thought

Lyons, hesitating an instant. But the man pulled a pistol from his belt holster. Even as Lyons snapped off two shots, a second ultrahigh-velocity slug slammed the biker into the asphalt. Lyons spoke into the radio again:

"Keep watch. If we got time, I'm going to strip those creeps."

"Role camouflage?"

"And transportation."

Blancanales was grinning as Lyons ran up to him. "Just the man I wanted to see."

His wired wrists hung from a bolt in the utility pole. Lyons lifted his friend off. Then he helped him untwist the wire.

"Can't you keep out of trouble?"

"Trouble is my business," Blancanales countered. He appeared unhurt from his ordeal, although his wrists were bleeding, and his head was badly banged up at the back, where he had received the rifle butt.

"Gadgets is up there." Lyons looked toward the top of the hill as he finished uncoiling the wire from Pol's wrists. "We got to get back there. A goon squad is coming this way. Which motorcycle you want?"

The hand-radio buzzed. "What's happening?" snapped Lyons.

"A car and three motorcycles, moving fast!"

"Let them come in the parking lot, fire when we do."

Lyons grabbed the G-3 from the asphalt and threw it to Blancanales, who had already regained his hijacked Beretta. Then he jerked the dead biker into a sitting position against a motorcycle. He pulled the messy heart-shot biker up against the utility pole where Blancanales had hung, and left the dead man sitting there, still leaking dark fluids. He went to the last biker, rolled him over to take his jacket, had to look away. Nausea twisted his gut.

Not looking at the part that had been a face before the accelerator got to it, Lyons stripped off the jacket. He dumped the body in the bushes. He found a chromed Nazi helmet, flipped it on, then sat on a Harley to wait, nonchalantly wiping bits of human tissue from the denim jacket.

Escorted by three low-slung motorcycles, a Lincoln Continental fishtailed into the parking lot and came to a tire-smoking stop. The Harleys swung in a wide loop, coming to a slower stop. Lyons waited.

A hoodlum resplendent in chrome-studded black leather jacket and pants stepped out of the Lincoln. He wore a western holster with a nickel-plated, pearl-handled six-gun. He looked at Lyons, lifted his sunglasses. "Who the fuck—"

"Surprise!"

Leaving the gravel road behind them, Able Team followed a rutted, four-wheel drive track several hundred yards into the hills on their captured Harleys. Blancanales pointed to a grassy area shaded by a sheer hillside. They coasted to a stop and propped the motorcycles against the embankment. Lyons looked back. They could not be seen from the main road.

"So, gentlemen, what's the plan? Where do we hit next?"

"I don't think our next engagement will be so easy," Blancanales said. He spread out his map of Catalina Island on the grass.

"Able Team eight, Outlaws zero," Lyons said without emotion.

"—but now they know we're here."

"I want you guys to hear something." Gadgets took the scanner/auto-recorder from his pack and re-wound the cassette. "The name of the Outlaws' leader is Horse. That's what the LAPD file said, and all the calls I've heard, the name of the man giving the orders is Horse. But listen to this."

He touched the play button. "Horse, this is your friend. Answer." "Yessir! This is Horse. Is there anything you need?" "No, everything's fine. I'm quite comfortable. Brief me...."

Gadgets played the conversation through. "That went out on a different frequency. What does it sound like to you?"

"Sounds like this isn't all Horse's game," Lyons replied. "He's just the front man."

"Is he talking with someone off the island?" Blancanales was fieldstripping the Beretta, spreading out the components on the plastic map. When the Outlaws had captured him, they had experimented with the weapon. He was checking it thoroughly, cleaning it like it had been violated.

"Maybe on a boat," Gadgets pondered. "But hardly the mainland. No way."

"So we have some mastermind floating offshore directing this horror show..." Lyons said. "You think all this could be a grab at those six scientists? By commies, terrorists? Except that that guy speaks perfect English. He couldn't be foreign."

"Too perfect," Blancanales said. "Remember, those eggheads are here by chance. They wanted a quiet place, this was close. They could've gone to

Lake Tahoe. The man talked about 'the seizure of the island,' and about money. If he only wanted those six, why not grab just them? Why take everyone on the island?''

"Yeah, very curious.'' Gadgets fast-forwarded the tape, stopping to listen to snatches of conversation.

"What else you got?'' Lyons asked.

"I don't know. Been kind of busy, haven't had a chance to listen—''

He caught another snatch of the calm, educated voice. ''—I can't help you there, Horse. Do what you think is necessary.''

Gadgets rewound the tape and found the beginning of this later conversation. "Any developments, Horse?'' "Yeah, more trouble with heroes. I've lost a couple of men to local crazies.'' "Your men can eliminate the opposition. Has there been any attempt yet to land security forces?'' "I don't know. There was nothing on the radar, but one of my men says they've got a commando over on the other side of the island.'' "Is that in fact true? If the authorities have ignored your stipulations....'' "We'll know soon enough. I'm going to, ah, put the questions to him myself. I've sent some men to bring him here. If he's a cop—'' "You will need to impress the authorities. If he is one of these local residents, I suggest you make an example of him.'' "Oh, yeah!'' "I'll call you again—'' "Wait, sir. I need to be able to call you.'' "Please don't. There is no privacy here. You could compromise me.'' "Yessir, I'm sorry sir.'' "Speak with you again in an hour.''

They heard Horse again: "Blackie. Come in! You got that commando? Blackie!''

Lyons now wore the biker's black leather jacket. "Sorry, Horse. Blackie is Missing In Action," he said under his breath.

Finished with the Beretta, Blancanales field-stripped and cleaned the captured Heckler and Koch G-3. "As long as they don't identify us," Blancanales reasoned, "we don't have to worry about the bikers taking it out on the hostages."

"What do you make of what he said?" Gadgets asked suddenly. "He said, 'There is no privacy here. You could compromise me.'"

Lyons counted off the points on his fingers. "One, he isn't alone. Two, the people he's with don't know what he's doing. Three, he isn't a resident. He used the words, 'one of these local residents,' right? He said it like he thought they were a lower life form. Four, we don't have time for a mystery. I say we hit the airport, the radio station, and every Outlaw patrol and outpost we can find. What do you two think?"

"Why the airport?" Blancanales asked. "He's got the place radar tight, nothing can come in."

"It gives the Feds and the LAPD an option. If we don't make it, they could land assault squads if things got desperate—"

"If we took out the radar!" Gadgets pointed to Mount Black Jack on Blancanales' map. "Right there. The radar station's in town, but the actual scanning equipment's up on top of this mountain. We hit that equipment, he's blind."

"Can't do it." Lyons shook his head. "Assault units would be a desperate, last-chance gamble. And hitting the radar wouldn't help. He'd pull in his men, kill the hostages before the assault teams got into town.

"And another problem. We are not making informed decisions. We won't be able to devise a real plan until we know what's out there. Time to move."

"Time to forward all this information to Brognola," Gadgets added. "Maybe Stonyman and the LAPD can work out a plan."

Lyons paced the dirt road while Gadgets prepared his transmission. Dictating into the recorder, Gadgets detailed what Able Team had seen and heard. He summarized their discussion on a possible coordinated assault. Then, plugging in the scrambler module and speeding up the tape to ten times normal, he transmitted the information. Anyone intercepting Gadgets' transmission would hear only a shriek of electronic noise. Finally Gadgets packed his equipment:

"Ready to go."

Blancanales gave the captured G-3 a last wipe, snapped in a magazine. "Loaded."

Lyons stared out at the dry hills rolling west to the Pacific. Steadily, a wide grin grew on his face:

"Gentlemen, I have the perfect plan. Simple, straightforward, very effective."

"What's that?" Gadgets asked.

"We kill them all."

8

Crowning the mountainous interior of Catalina, the Airport in the Sky equalled its name. The engineers who had created this marvel of beauty and utility leveled the peaks of a mountain range to sculpt an artificial plateau high above the island. The airfield viewed the surrounding island, the vast Pacific to the west, the San Pedro Channel to the east, and when the winds blew away the smog of Los Angeles, the hundred miles of coast where the metropolis met the ocean.

Resident commuters, regardless of how often they flew in and out, enjoyed every flight. To the islanders returning from the concrete and glass maze of Los Angeles, the landing field seemed to be a platform floating between the blue-domed heaven of the sky and the primitive paradise of their isolated home. To the uninitiated tourist arriving from the mainland, their flight's descent to the field provided the first thrilling vision of an island wonderland known for its unique natural beauty.

Even those tourists who come to the island by boat often included the Airport in the Sky in their schedule, leaving the island's only town in buses and rented cars and following the winding, back-switching road through canyons and hills to the high airfield.

Able Team followed the same road, but did not continue to the man-made plateau of the airport. They stopped short. After studying their topographical maps of the island, they concealed their commandeered motorcycles and hiked up a steep gorge to the flat mountain crest.

At the top, on their bellies in the dry brush, they saw the Early California-style airport facilities two hundred yards to the north. They scanned the exteriors and the windows and doorways of the buildings with binoculars and the eight-power scope of the Mannlicher sniper rifle.

They saw silhouetted movements within the glass-walled controller's booth in the three-story tower.

"Three bikes outside," Lyons told the others. He raised the Mannlicher slightly. "Only two Outlaws in the tower."

"Outlaw number three," Gadgets said, "is in the chair on the restaurant patio."

Lyons scanned the parking lot, the restaurant, the control tower. "I say we go straight through the front door."

"Second the motion," Blancanales agreed. He chambered a round in the Beretta.

Staying below the edge of the plateau, they followed the contour of the mountain until they were downslope from the parking lot. Staying flat as they crawled up, they peered through the decorative bushes and flowers of the landscaping. Unlike the mountainsides, the restaurant landscaping was watered and tended through all the seasons, and it stayed spring green. The lush growth provided cover.

The sentry, his walkie-talkie on the patio bricks

beside him, sat only a hundred feet away. Lyons
pointed to himself and Gadgets, then pointed to the
airport buildings. He pointed to Blancanales, then
pointed to the sentry and pulled an imaginary trigger.
Blancanales nodded.

Holding the Beretta in both hands, Blancanales extended the pistol in front of him at arm's length,
resting both his elbows and the butt of the pistol on
the ground. He sighted on the biker's chest as Lyons
and Gadgets pushed up into sprinter's starting
stance.

A voice cracked from the walkie-talkie. As Blancanales fired, the sentry leaned down to pick up the
hand-radio. The sub-sonic 9mm slug slapped into his
jacket sleeve. Forgetting the radio, he looked at the
small hole, watched blood run from his arm. Then he
saw Lyons and Gadgets charging at him.

He reached through scorching pain for the pistol at
his belt, then he jerked back in the chair, a three-
round burst punching a pattern into his chest. But he
still moved, half rising from the chair as he groped
for his pistol with his left hand. A final silent bullet
hit him in the forehead. He sat back, his face slack,
his three eyes open. The radio squawked again:

"Hey, goofball. Answer the radio. This is Eagle."

Lyons picked up the hand-radio and pressed the
talk button. "Yeah?"

Gadgets pressed himself against the restaurant's
stucco wall, looked for Lyons, saw him listening to
the hand-radio as he rearranged the dead biker's
body. He was positioning the dead man to look like
he had fallen asleep, his face resting on his shoulder.

"I want you down where you can watch that road,

you hear me?'' the radio voice continued. ''I don't
want you in the restaurant drinking the beer, I don't
want you wandering around smoking dope, I want
you watching that road. Horse said—''

''Horse said shit,'' Lyons sneered into the radio.
He saw Gadgets watching wide-eyed. Lyons grinned.
''You don't tell me nothing.''

''What? What did you say? You want me to come
down there and kick your ass right off this island?''

''Waiting for you.''

''You piece of—'' The voice cut off.

Lyons left the radio in the dead man's hands, then
ran over to the stucco wall. He stood on the other
side of the restaurant's door from Gadgets. Gadgets
grinned, shook his head. Lyons waved his arms to get
Blancanales' attention, then pointed at the restaurant
door. They waited.

Thirty seconds later, the plate glass door flew
open, slamming into Lyons where he stood against
the wall. His Ingram banged the glass.

Looking at the biker who stomped out, they knew
why he was called Eagle. His nose stuck out two
inches from his face, the bridge of it almost perpen-
dicular to his forehead, the end hooking down. And
like an eagle, people looked up to him. He stood six-
foot-eight.

Hearing the metallic clang of Lyons' Ingram on
the plate glass, he glanced behind the door. For a big
man, he moved fast, whipping the door aside, then
driving a kick at Lyons' groin.

Both hands braced on the small weapon, Lyons
blocked the kick with his Ingram. The kick bounced
him off the wall. Eagle lunged for him.

A slug zipped past Eagle and smashed the glass door. Lyons' throat in one hand, his fist drawn back to smash this blond stranger in an Outlaws jacket, Eagle saw Gadgets bringing up his Uzi.

Eagle bashed Gadgets with Lyons. Gadgets sprawled on the bricks, the Uzi flying from his hand. Still holding Lyons by the throat, Eagle whipped an eighteen-inch machete from his belt.

Jamming the Ingram's stubby barrel against the biker's gut, Lyons fired a burst, five 9mm Parabellum slugs ripping through the man. They exited from his back and side.

Eagle didn't let go of Lyons. He raised the heavy blade to hack away the ex-cop's head. Lyons fired again, then again, swinging the muzzle back and forth as if he fought with a chain saw. He emptied the Ingram through the biker. Thirty slugs cut huge red slashes through his gut and chest.

The machete slipped from his hand finally, as he toppled backward and died.

A pair of boots in panic ran across the roof of the restaurant. Lyons fell back against the wall, gasping. He dropped the magazine out of the Ingram. He struggled to fit in another. A dazed Gadgets snatched up his Uzi, aimed up. But he had no target.

"Eagle! What's that shooting?" a voice above them demanded. "Hey, man! Move your ass! Someone's shooting—"

The G-3 boomed from the parking lot's flowering hedge. The body of a biker tumbled from the roof, fell to the bricks.

Lyons leaned against the restaurant wall, sucking breaths through his aching throat; Gadgets straightened his Outlaws jacket, checked his Uzi for damage.

That all was close.

It left them both really pissed off.

Following Forest Service roads and firebreaks, the three warriors on their Outlaw Harley 1200s weaved their way through the interior of the island. From time to time they could see the antennas of Radio Station KCAT on Mount Black Jack, where KCAT shared the peak with the Harbor Master's radar installation. A final bumpy motorcycle climb up a canyon's dry stream bed took them halfway up Mount Black Jack, to within a thousand feet of the station. They could go no farther on the bikes without risking observation.

Lyons sprinted to a ridge crest and watched the station through the scope of the Mannlicher. While the ex-cop was gone, Gadgets conferred with Blancanales:

"You know why that mess happened at the airport?"

Blancanales nodded.

Gadgets continued. "We've got to come to an agreement with Lyons about improvising. He's taking a lot of long, long chances. He's going to run out of luck. You stand with me?"

"If he goes down, we lose a very good man."

Lyons came toward them, returning from the ridge. "One man on the roof with binoculars. He's smoking dope and throwing beer cans. Ready to go?"

"No," Gadgets told him. "I declare a 'Severe Self-Criticism Session.' You came within a second of dying back there at the airport. If super-creep had come out with a weapon in his hands, you'd be dead. From now on, we *plan* it, then we do it. No more improvising."

Thinking only a moment, Lyons nodded. "At the time it seemed the right thing to do, faking him out on the hand-radio. It wasn't. I'm sorry. I was grandstanding. I am self-criticized. Now we go?"

Able Team proceeded to the peak of Mount Black Jack along narrow slashes of erosion, the overfolding brush obscuring the sky and the possible observation of the sentry above them.

Creeping to the edge of the fire-clearing around the station, they saw the cinder block buildings with open balconies that housed the offices and transmitter of KCAT, and a few hundred yards farther along a dirt road there was a steel tower supporting the constantly rotating scanners of the Harbor Master's radar. Outside the door of the radio offices, a hundred-yards away, were two Honda Cross Country Cruisers.

"I don't want to try a hundred-yard shot with the Beretta," Blancanales said. "Next time the sentry wanders over to the other side, I'll sprint for the door. You guys cover me, then the three of us bust in. Agreed? Enough of a plan?"

The others nodded, smiling. Blancanales waited, then ran. At the door, he pressed against the wall. The door hung ajar. It had been shot open. Above him, he heard the crunch of motorcycle boots.

A beer can fell, rolled on the concrete of the balcony, foam and beer gushing from the top. "Goddamn it," the biker muttered. Then he called out as he leaned over the edge. "Vito. Throw up another beer—"

"Coming up." Blancanales called, a single slug suddenly punching into the biker's nose. He collapsed, his hand and head twitching as they hung over the edge of the parapet. Lyons and Gadgets joined Blancanales.

Blancanales pointed to himself, then pointed inside. Lyons shielded himself with the Ingram as they stepped into the office.

The room was empty. Blancanales continued to the next door, Lyons a step behind him.

In front of a television, a very pale biker nodded off. He wore only undershirt and jeans. In one hand he was holding a length of surgical tubing. A needle and syringe hung from his other arm. He didn't wake from his heroin stupor as Blancanales slipped up to him, put the Beretta to his temple. The junkie would never wake.

They returned to the door. "It's all over."

"Now we go put this—" Gadgets held up a small charge of C-4 explosive with a radio detonator. "—on the radar."

"I'll do the clean-up here," Lyons offered. I'll be watching the road down the hill until you get back."

Gadgets and Blancanales nodded, then hurried out. Lyons gathered together the junkie's jacket, boots, and World War II German MP-40 submachinegun. He dumped the whole lot, dead junkie and belongings, into a tangle of brush outside.

He heard the motorcycles before he saw them. Running back to the station office, he keyed his hand-radio: "Gadgets, Pol! Take cover, bikers coming up."

"There's a sentry on the radar tower!" Gadgets hissed. "We're stuck out in the open hoping he won't—Oh, man... he sees us. We are in the shit!"

The Outlaws' walkie-talkie buzzed. Behind the voice, there was the roar of engines. "On our way up to relieve you dudes. I tell you, you're going to dig the good times at the casino—hey, you mother-fuckers! You shooting at us?"

Rifle fire was ripping the quiet. A confusion of voices on the Outlaws' walkie-talkie mixed with the motorcycles' roar as they gunned up the hill. Lyons looked out the door, saw four bikers race past. Half-way between the radio station and the radar towers, Gadgets and Blancanales sprawled in the dirt road's ruts. A biker on the radar towers fired down at them with a large caliber rifle.

Firing wild from the handlebars of their 1200s, the four bikers sprayed Gadgets and Blancanales with shotgun and automatic fire. Bullets and double-zero shot kicked up dust all around Gadgets and Blanca-nales. The sniper in the towers continued firing.

A burst from Gadgets' Uzi spilled one of the bikers. Lyons grabbed the Outlaw walkie-talkie. "Pull back to the radio station! Chief's coming up the hill with twenty more guys. Don't die for noth-ing. We'll sit back here and shoot those two assholes to pieces."

Lyons saw the bikers circling back. He snatched an extra magazine for his Ingram. He stood in the door-way in his biker clothing, with the walkie-talkie covering most of his face. When the three bikers came within twenty feet, ignorant of the danger, he emptied his Ingram at them, knocking down two, wounding the third. Lyons ducked behind the cinder block wall, slammed in the second magazine, then blasted the third biker as he dumped his motorcycle and tried to pump a shotgun with an injured arm. Another biker, badly wounded, struggled to crawl behind his bike for cover, but died as slugs ripped away pieces of his head, punching holes in his downed bike. Gasoline whooshed into a dramatic fireball, singeing Lyons' eyebrows.

Changing magazines again, Lyons put a coup de grace burst through the third biker. On the other end of the mountain crest, Uzi and G-3 fire answered the sentry's rifle. Lyons saw the sentry fall through the tower struts.

Sprinting, Lyons didn't pause as he fired a burst through the spilled biker in front of him. The smell of death was everywhere. He continued on to Gadgets and Blancanales.

"Great trick, grandstand." Blancanales rose out of the dust holding his thigh.

"Heard it on the walkie-talkie," Gadgets grinned.

"Sorry about that," Lyons laughed. "Did it again. Improvised."

"I didn't say you couldn't improvise when it was necessary—"

"Pol, you're wounded." Lyons saw blood on Blancanales.

"My G-3 got customized." The automatic rifle had two bullet holes in the plastic buttstock. "And my leg, too. But—" He pulled a Heckler and Koch box magazine out of his thigh pocket. Bent and twisted, the magazine had a hole through it. Blancanales reached into his pocket again, felt the wound, probed it. "Oww! Here it is, double-ought." He held up the flattened lead ball.

"You okay, Gadgets?" Lyons asked.

"Oh, yeah. I took cover behind Pol!"

The screech of the Outlaws' walkie-talkie interrupted them: "This is Stonewall, come in Horse. We're a couple of blocks up from the pier, and we got ourselves a hero. Alive." Horse's coarse laughter cackled through the walkie-talkie: "Bring him in. We'll make an example of him."

The three fatigued but fit Able Team avengers looked to one another. "Anything we can do?" Lyons asked.

"In Avalon?" Blancanales shook his head, no.

Carl Lyons looked at the ground. "Well, God grant you a quick death, whoever you are."

9

Minutes before dawn, Glen and Ann Shepard, the Davis cousins, and Jack Webster slipped out of the Davis home. They crossed the street, went through a yard, climbed a fence. Rather than risk crossing the next street, they climbed fence after fence until they came to the end of the block. They broke into the last home in the street, a two-story house with a peaked roof.

Waiting there, they heard shots and yells and roaring motorcycles. As the Outlaws swept the other block, smashing doors and rampaging through homes, Glen examined the home in which they were hiding. As he had thought when he first saw the house, there was a triangular crawl space between the ceiling of the second floor and the peak of the steeply angled roof. He found the access hole in the ceiling of one bedroom's closet. He helped his wife up—her eighth-month belly a tight squeeze—then passed up blankets, water, a transistor radio with an earphone, all the weapons, and a plastic bucket to serve as a toilet.

Glen and the boys carefully searched through the drawers and closets of the house. He told the boys they would be hiding in the attic all day and perhaps the night, however long the siege of the island continued. They should gather anything that would make their wait more pleasant or safer. He also advised them to return everything they touched to where it had been. The house must not appear different than when they entered.

From the vents of the attic, they watched the Outlaws search the nearby homes. The Outlaws did not discover the knifed Acidhead until an hour after dawn. The crackle of the radiophones and walkie-talkies reached a pitch approaching hysteria. The discovery of the corpse, with rifle, pistol, ammunition and radiophone gone, had gotten the Outlaws seriously fired up.

Hearing motorcycles and voices getting really close outside, Roger went to a vent and peeked through the louvers. "They're searching this block now."

"Don't sweat it," Glen spoke calmly. "Roger, stay there, watch the street. Chris, you go to that back vent, watch the back. Both of you take blankets."

"Why?" asked Chris.

"Because if they open up the trapdoor and look in here," Glen explained, "if it's dark, they won't be able to see us: If we hear them in the closet down there, you cover those vents with the blankets. But dig it—once they come in the house, nobody moves! Have those blankets folded up and ready so you can do it silently."

"What if they have flashlights?" Roger asked.

"Then we got a problem."

"And what should I do?" asked Jack.

"Go over there," Glen pointed to a far corner of the attic. "Lie in the corner and be quiet. Ann, you go over there, put that dark blanket over you. I'll try to make myself invisible too.''

Glen pressed himself into a small space between a rising vent pipe and the roof joists. He pointed his sawed-off shotgun at the access door.

"I'll shoot when you do," Jack told him. Glen looked over, saw the .45 auto in Jack's hands.

Putting down his shotgun, Glen crouch-walked over to Jack. "Give me the pistol."

"Why? It's mine."

"It isn't yours," Chris called out. "Give it to Mr. Shepard."

For an instant, Glen thought the teenager would shoot him. Then he saw that the hammer was only at half-cock. He grabbed the pistol, twisted it from the boy's hands.

"I'm taking this weapon," Glen told him, "because you having it is a threat to our lives. All you've been talking about is shooting them, and if you did that they'd kill us all.

"You asshole!" Jack shouted. "You're no one to me, you can't play God with me, I'll—"

One-handed, Glen grabbed the teenager by the throat and started to choke him. "Be quiet!" he hissed. "You'll get us killed."

Roger whispered from the far end of the attic. "Do what he tells you, jerk-off! You should be thanking him. He risked his life to help us."

"Shut the fuck up, nigger!" Jack screamed at Roger.

"Ohhhhhh . . ." Glen just laughed. "Is this guy your friend?"

"Will you shut up?" Chris hissed. "They're out there!"

Crouch-walking again, Glen went to the vent viewing the street. "Where?"

"Coming around the corner. He isn't really a friend of ours, by the way," Chris explained quietly to Glen. "We sorta know him. He was hanging around, when all this started."

"When it's over, why don't you and your cousin kick that punk's ass? Until then, we'd better watch him carefully. Here they come."

"They're in the neighbor's backyard!" Roger gulped.

Glen and Chris watched the Outlaws search the houses.

They kicked down doors, broke windows. Dogs barked. Shots silenced them.

A new group of bikers roared up on their Harleys, Kawasakis, Hondas, led by the barrel-chested Outlaw in the Confederate Army cap. He wore a shotgun slung over his shoulder. A long bayonet flashed in the morning light. The group continued to the house where Acidhead had died; they parked their bikes there, and went in.

A pistol popped in the house next to where they hid. Three bikers dragged an elderly man and woman from the house. Outlaws converged on the scene. The elderly man—white-haired and stick thin—comforted his wife as bikers crowded around them, taunting the old man.

The biker in the Rebel cap swaggered up and glared at the old man. One of the bikers who had dragged out the couple showed the Rebel-capped biker a small pistol, then pointed to a rip in his jacket sleeve. The Confederate biker unslung his shotgun.

"Oh, God," Chris gasped, turning away from the vent. "I can't watch this."

"Watch it," Glen told him. "It's what'll happen to you, to all of·us if we get caught."

"Run, you old geezer!" the Outlaw suddenly boomed. "You want to escape. Here's your chance!"

Glen looked outside. The bikers cleared a path for the couple. A biker shoved them. The Confederate Outlaw stood with the shotgun at his hip, pointing at the old couple only six feet away.

The white-haired old man shook his head. He refused to run. He held his wife, pressing her face to his chest. He kissed her forehead.

A single blast threw them to the asphalt. They sprawled together, a huge blood pool spreading around them.

"Now they're coming to search this house," Glen told the others.

"Hey, Stonewall!" a biker on the street called out. "You are one cold mother." Several bikers laughed.

Glen peeked out, saw the Rebel-capped biker loading shells into his shotgun. Now Glen knew the biker's name: Stonewall.

"Think that's cold?" the biker shouted. "I'm looking for the hero that killed one of ours. When I find him.... You all see this cap? When I'm done with that hero, I'm going to wear his hide for a hat—right up here, nose and eyes and lips and all, just like a coonskin cap."

More laughter. Boots kicked down the door. Shotgun blasts inside the house shattered windows, sent furniture crashing. They must have been doing this to every house on the island. Bikers shouted:

"Where are you? Get out of this house! All we want's your money and valuables. And we want you down at the Casino. Anybody in here, come out. We want you with the other people."

Laughter. Rifle shots ripped through the house. A shotgun blast smashed a wall beneath them; a single pellet popped through the rafters, then bounced off the roof joists.

"Glen," his wife whispered. "come be here with me...."

"I can't!" he hissed.

Boots stormed up the stairs. Doors slammed open, furniture fell. A voice shouted: "Check every closet!"

The blast of a shotgun. Plaster exploding upward. "That closet's checked!" Laughter.

"Rings! Diamonds. Hey, asshole. Split it with me."

"They're mine. Find your own."

"Both of you!" Stonewall's voice boomed. "Stick that trash in your pockets. Search this house. You got two dead buddies and you're fighting over some phony rings? Search that closet, under the bed, up in the attic, everywhere!

"Psst!" Glen hissed to Roger. Then he and Chris blocked the vent near them. The attic went pitch dark.

Furniture crashed down. The closet door leading to the attic access creaked open. Shoes and suitcases fell from the shelves.

"Hey, there's a trapdoor going up," a biker said.

"You going up there?"

"Going up. First, some reconnaissance by fire!"

An explosion of plaster, insulation, and splintered wood filled the attic. Sudden light flashed as the debris flew. Dim light glowed through the several holes in the access panel and closet ceiling.

As the biker pushed up the splintered access panel, Glen could hear Roger's breathing shudder slightly. But he could do nothing. He could not encourage or comfort the teenager. A word or a sound would betray them all.

The biker's head appeared above the rafters, swivelling in all directions. "Hey, you! You! I see you...."

"You got one?" a biker called from below.

Glen heard Chris stop breathing. Slowly, very slowly, Glen grasped the butt of the Magnum in his belt. Outside, bikers laughed and shouted. A motorcycle raced down the street.

The head dropped down. "Nah, nothing up there."

Stonewall shouted again. "Move it! We got this whole block to search. Find anything?"

"Nah," the biker answered, the last to leave the house.

"Then move it! Find that hero! Horse is going to waste my ass if I don't come up with that bastard."

Glen glanced out front, saw the last biker leave the house and start down the block. Stonewall came out of the house, shotgun ready, its long bayonet flashing. He turned, stared at the house. He saw the attic vent, stared at it. From the hip, he pointed the shotgun, fired.

1. How do you rate _____ ?
   (Please print book TITLE)

   1.6 ☐ excellent   .4 ☐ good   .2 ☐ not so good
   .5 ☐ very good   .3 ☐ fair   .1 ☐ poor

   (vertical at right margin: 9 8 7 6 5 4 3 2 1 D)

2. How likely are you to purchase another book in this series?

   2.1 ☐ definitely would purchase   .3 ☐ probably would not purchase
   .2 ☐ probably would purchase   .4 ☐ definitely would not purchase

3. How do you compare this title with similar books you usually read?

   3.1 ☐ far better than others   .4 ☐ not as good
   .2 ☐ better than others   .5 ☐ definitely not as good
   .3 ☐ about the same

4. Have you any additional comments about this book?

   _____ (4)
   _____ (6)

5. How did you first become aware of this book?

   8. ☐ in-store display   11. ☐ talk show
   9. ☐ radio   12. ☐ read Executioner books
   10. ☐ magazine _____   13. ☐ other _____
   (name)   (please specify)

6. What most prompted you to buy this book?

   14. ☐ title   17. ☐ picture on cover   20. ☐ back-cover story outline
   15. ☐ price   18. ☐ friend's recommendation   21. ☐ read a few pages
   16. ☐ author   19. ☐ product advertising   22. ☐ other _____
   (please specify)

7. How do you usually obtain your books?

   23. ☐ bookstore   26. ☐ department/discount store   29. ☐ borrow
   24. ☐ drugstore   27. ☐ convenience store   30. ☐ other
   25. ☐ supermarket   28. ☐ subscription
   (please specify)

8. What type(s) of paperback fiction have you purchased in the past 3 months? Approximately how many?

	No. purchased		No. purchased
☐ contemporary romance	(31)_____	☐ espionage	(45)_____
☐ historical romance	(33)_____	☐ western	(47)_____
☐ gothic romance	(35)_____	☐ contemporary novels	(49)_____
☐ romantic suspense	(37)_____	☐ historical novels	(51)_____
☐ mystery	(39)_____	☐ science fiction/fantasy	(53)_____
☐ private eye	(41)_____	☐ occult	(55)_____
☐ action/adventure	(43)_____	☐ other	(57)_____

9. On which date was this book purchased? (59) _____

10. Please indicate your age group and sex.

    61.1 ☐ Male   62.1 ☐ under 15   .3 ☐ 25-34   .5 ☐ 50-64
    .2 ☐ Female   .2 ☐ 15-24   .4 ☐ 35-49   .6 ☐ 65 or older

Thank you for completing and returning this questionnaire.

NAME _____
                    (Please Print)
ADDRESS _____
CITY _____
ZIP CODE _____

BUSINESS REPLY MAIL

FIRST CLASS   PERMIT NO. 70   TEMPE, AZ.

POSTAGE WILL BE PAID BY ADDRESSEE

NATIONAL READER SURVEYS

1440 SOUTH PRIEST DRIVE
TEMPE, AZ. 85281

Glen jerked Chris away as the louvers exploded. Light streamed into the attic. For a half minute, Glen and Chris lay without moving on the rafters.

"Glen!" his wife whispered.

"I'm all right," he gasped. He went back to the shattered louvers and snuck a peek. The front lawn was deserted.

They listened. In the house, there was only silence. But in the house next door, there were shouts and shots and crashing.

"Mr. Shepard," Roger whispered from the far end. "Can I let down the blanket now? I'm shot."

"What?" Glen crept over the rafters, crab-style, moving slowly and silently. As he passed his wife, he hugged her, gave her a quick kiss. Continuing, when he passed Jack Webster, he smelled fecal matter, heard the boy's teeth chattering with fear. Glen said nothing.

A single double-zero ball had punched through Roger's right forearm. There was a hole in the blanket that he had held over the vent, then a hole in the wall stud. Roger had obviously held the blanket over the vent for minutes after taking the through-and-through wound in his arm.

"Oh, god, it hurts," Roger sobbed.

Glen put his arm around the teenager's shoulders. "That's all right. You saved us. You're the hero of this battle. That Aryan punk over there talks tough, but when the going gets rough, he shits his pants."

"You fucker!" Jack shrieked. He lunged across the narrow attic, snatching the .45 auto from where Glen had left it. Glen pulled the Magnum from his belt. But the boy didn't turn the weapon on Glen. Instead, he grabbed the M-14 too, and the ammo bandolier, and disappeared down the access hatch.

"Jack! I'm sorry! Don't go out there." Glen stumbled to the hatch, but Jack Webster was gone. Glen grasped his belt of bullets and started after the boy.

"Glen, don't!" his wife called.

"Let him go, Mr. Shepard," Chris pleaded.

"It was my big mouth," Glen called back. "They'll take him if I don't get to him first. I don't want it on my conscience."

Glen Shepard dropped through the blast-splintered hatch.

10

Crying with shame and rage, Jack Webster ran from the back of the savaged house. He heard shots and voices in the houses down the block, motorcycles on the streets. Not wanting to chance going over the back fence, he slipped into the decorative hedges screening one yard from the other. For a minute or two, he lay there on his stomach, his face pressed into the rotting leaves, and cried.

But the rifle in his grip reassured him. "I'll show them. I'll kill some of them."

Hidden by the hedge, he crawled along the fence, searching for a hole. The rotting wood slats crumbled when he touched them, but the neighbor's chain link prevented him from crawling through. He continued to the corner of the yard.

In the corner, dogs had burrowed under the fences. The dog holes had been blocked with bricks. Jack pulled out the bricks, crawled under the fence, coming out in the backyard of the house diagonally behind the house where the others still hid.

The shooting continued as the Outlaws searched. Jack crawled through the untrimmed bushes of the backyard until he came to the back door. The door hung open, a ragged hole where the knob and lock had been. Crouching there for minutes, he listened for voices or steps inside the house. He heard nothing. Struggling to work the rifle's action, he jerked back the cocking lever. A cartridge flew out.

He marvelled at the size of the cartridge. He had only fired .22 rifles before. The bullet was huge. He put the .308 NATO round in his pocket. Holding the rifle at his hip and his finger on the trigger like he'd seen in the movies, he crept into the house.

Broken dishes littered the kitchen floor. He slid his feet over the linoleum, gingerly pushing the fragments of glass and china away rather than step on them. Once onto the dining room and living room rugs, he walked quickly to the front windows.

Down the street a few addresses, he saw the Davis house. The front door hung by one hinge. Looking up and down the other side of the street, he saw all the front doors had been kicked in or shot open.

Creeping to the blasted front door of the house, Jack eased it closed, then carefully blocked the door with a heavy cabinet. He went to the back door, blocked it also.

Sure he couldn't be surprised, he searched the house. In one of the bedrooms, he found clothes almost his size. He changed his stinking pants. The evidence of his fear and shame gone, he felt bolder.

He found jewelry, wristwatches, and money. He wore the man's wristwatch, pocketed the other loot. In the children's room, he found a knapsack. He filled the pack with food, soda pop, and a bottle of vodka from the kitchen. Then he had a breakfast of white bread and sandwich meats.

"This ain't a bad time at all," he laughed. After

breakfast, when there was no further sight and sound of bikers, he looted all the other houses on the street.

Glen Shepard couldn't find the boy. He searched all the rooms of the house, the garage, then the backyard. He didn't risk the street or the other houses on the block. He couldn't believe Jack would have been so stupid as to go into the street. Finally, Glen returned to the others.

"Anything on the walkie-talkie?" he asked, clambering into the attic.

"Glen," Ann seethed, "you talk about responsibility? What about me? What about these kids? One minute you're ready to kill that jerk, the next you're out trying to save him. Why don't you worry about your own child? You're so dumb—you think just because you're right, just because you're the true believer...." Her anger became sobbing.

"Okay, okay," he whispered, "you're right. Forget that punk.... If they haven't got him yet, he can take care of himself. Because I tell you, just walking down there scares the shit out of me!"

He tried to make his voice sound patient, if not serene. "Roger, how's your arm?"

"It hurts."

"A month from now you'll have a scar to show your girl friends. Chris, what did you see?"

"Bikers. What's going on down below?"

"I think the radio will tell us more than anything we can see. What did you hear?"

"Something happened on the other side of the island. They said they caught a commando. They sent a bunch of bikers to bring him back to town, but they disappeared.''

"The commandos?"

"No, the bikers!"

"All right! Help is on its way. This'll all be over soon. Oh, God. I want it over right now. Will you two keep watch for a while, listen to the walkie-talkie?"

"You're not going anywhere!" Ann told him. "You promised."

"Going to sleep! Only to sleep." He lay down beside his very pregnant wife and held her, one arm across her belly. "And you too, mother-to-be. Last night wasn't too restful for us. For the three of us."

Sunbathing on the flat roof of a two-story house, Jack smoked dope, drank vodka. He was rich. He had found jewelry, gold coins, rolls of ten-dollar bills, platinum wristwatches. After the island returned to normal, Jack would shuttle back and forth to the mainland, selling a few things at a time. Theft was not new to him. That was how he paid for his Hawaiian grass and his new surfboards. When he stole from tourists and burglarized homes, he disposed of the articles through connections in Los Angeles. He hoped his connection could raise the thousands of dollars the loot was worth.

Motorcycles passed. The Outlaws! Wow, if he were an Outlaw, he'd have it made. They got the best stuff. He got what was left. If he were an Outlaw, he'd play it smart. Take the island, get his share, then before the SWAT teams and Marines showed up, he'd steal a boat and sail away with the loot.

The sun warming his face, Jack worked it out. Hundreds of thousands of dollars in cash and jewelry. Gold and diamonds. Sailing the Pacific, selling the booty when he needed money. Living like a pirate. Wow, what a life.

Another long hit of Hawaiian brought the dream to life in color. Girls' brown bodies stretched out on the deck of the pirate's yacht. Riding the winds and waves forever.

Asshole Outlaws. What would they do with their money? Buy motorcycles. Live in Beverley Hills and strip their Harleys on the carpet.

What if he could take it away from them? What if he could shoot an Outlaw, take the dead biker's loot? What if he could shoot Outlaw after Outlaw? Then he could buy the yacht. And he could leave the island a hero, the kid who wiped out the Outlaws. He'd stash the loot, then claim the glory. Sail away.

He sucked down a last hit and gulped some vodka. He staggered with the M-14 to the edge of the roof. The frame of the boxy house continued eighteen inches above the asphalt of the roof, like a very low railing. He saw a drain hole through the wall. Laying down on the asphalt, he peered through the four inch by four inch hole. It viewed the far end of the block. If he shot through the hole, he could kill any biker at the other end of the block, and they couldn't even see him! The shots would come from nowhere. When he killed two or three, he'd sneak down there, take whatever cash and jewelry they had, then come up here and repeat it. He would have his yacht!

Still on his belly, he tried to put the barrel of the M-14 through the hole. The front sight caught on the stucco. Jack twisted the rifle to force it through the hole. His fingers touched the trigger.

A burst ripped the quiet neighborhood, the rifle jumping in his hand, slamming back against his bicep. He tried to jerk his hand away, another wild burst sent slugs punching into houses and parked cars.

Motorcycles raced down the block. They jumped the curb. Boots kicked down the front door.

Chris woke Glen. "Mr. Shepard, there was some shooting. And then the Outlaws talked on the radios. They said, 'Some young kid with Acidhead's M-14.' Then that Stonewall said, 'We got a hero, alive.' Then Horse says, 'Bring him in. We'll make an example of him.' I think it was Jack they got."

"Me too," Glen agreed.

"What do you think they'll do to him?"

Glen slipped on the belt of shotgun cartridges. "That's not what I'm worrying about."

Horse put his .45 to Jack's blond hair. "I didn't—I didn't shoot at your guys," Jack pleaded. "I dropped it and it went off. I was up there hiding out and I dropped it."

Keeping the muzzle of the automatic against the boy's head, Horse glanced to Stonewall. The barrel-chested biker stood behind the teenager, holding the knapsack full of money and jewelry they'd found on the roof with Jack. Stonewall shrugged.

"Then how come you had the rifle?" Horse continued, "if you weren't going to shoot my men."

"I took it from a house. I wanted it."

"What house?"

Jack told them.

Stonewall searched the attic himself. He found th. blankets, the soda pop cans, the bloodstains where one of the people hiding up there had been wounded. He reported to Horse:

"They're gone. We must have just missed them. These blankets are still warm. Man, just by two or three minutes."

"Search the neighborhood again," Horse ordered.

"They couldn't have gotten off the block." Stonewall turned and shouted to his men. "Burn it! Burn it all!"

"Okay, kid," Horse said to Jack. "You helped us. We missed them by just a couple of minutes. Now—"

"I told you. I didn't—"

"Punk! You want to live?"

Jack nodded.

"Now, punk, what I want you to do is help us some more. I'm going to take you to the Casino and put you in there with the rest of your people. We've been seeing some funny stuff going on in there. And I want you to tell me all about it. You're my Private Eye."

"What if—"

"What if what?"

"Nothing's going on."

"I told you, something's going on." Horse pulled out his knife. "Charlie, this kid don't learn. He's useless. Pull down his pants and hold him. I'm going to fix him.''

Thrashing in Charlie's grip, Jack screamed and pleaded. Horse held the eight-inch blade of the Bowie near the boy's naked crotch. "Now, I told you something's going on. You're going to find out what it is. We'll give you an hour. You don't have something to tell us, we'll stand you up on the ballroom bandstand and cut that little thing off of you. Do you unnerstan' now?''

Jack nodded, pulled up his pants.

With tears streaming down their faces, Jack's mother and father hugged him. It was the first time in his life he could remember emotion from them. "We thought you were dead."

"So did I. They're killing people out there."

The residents crowding around Jack questioned him:

"Did you see the Davis boys?"

"Did you see any police?"

Max Stevens pushed in front of the others. "We want you to tell us everything you saw and heard. It's very important to us."

"Why?" Jack asked. "What's going on?"

11

Descending Mount Black Jack on captured Harleys, Able Team returned to the dry streambed where they had concealed their equipment and other motorcycles. Lyons transferred his backpack and rifle case from the bike he'd seized after the campground ambush.

"I'm beginning to like this machine I've been riding," he told his partners. "It's a Harley classic. And the chrome and black lacquer sure go with my jacket, hey?"

"Topping off the tanks over here," Blancanales called out. "Don't dump any of the bikes without letting me siphon out—"

"Hey! They're at the airport," Gadgets yelled. He ran over to Blancanales and Lyons with a captured walkie-talkie. "Listen—"

The voices squawked back and forth. "...Eagle and the other two dudes are gone." "What? They dead? What's—" "Just gone. We searched the airport. There's no blood, nothing. Oh, yeah. One of the doors is broke. But there's nothing—" "Get over to the radio station. Ironman went up there with three men to change the guard and all kinds of shit broke loose. One of them said you were coming up the hill. Then it went quiet, nothing on the radio. Get over there fast!'' ''Horse, it's the locals. They're running circles around us. They know the territory. They're making like the Viet Cong—'' ''Dig this, Chief. You were the Marine. Get me a body count. Out!''

Opening his map of the island, Blancanales pointed to their position, then traced the route the bikers would take from the airport to the peak of Mount Black Jack. ''They'll take the main road to the radio station turnoff, then go up the hill. They're four miles away from that turnoff, we're only a mile. I say we hit them there.''

''What if it isn't right for an ambush?'' Lyons asked.

''We let them go up the hill, then we find a better place, hit them on the way down.''

''Let's move it!''

Moto-crossing, they left the canyon behind and found a wide hiking trail. Speeding until they dared go no faster, Able Team tore up the trail with their heavy semi-chopped Harleys, scraping fancy stone steps with their crankcases, rutting beds of rare California wild flowers.

They made it. Steep hillsides rose above the junction of the paved highway and the station's dirt road. The station's road cut along the south slope of canyon running east and west. Fifty feet up from the highway, a steel gate blocked the dirt road. Now it stood open, its lock shot away. Below the road, the hillside dropped ten feet to a streambed, the streambed ending at a grated culvert passing under the highway. For hundreds of yards north and south, the highway ran straight.

"Okay, Pol," Lyons said. "You're the Green Beret, retired. Call it."

Blancanales pointed to the ridge on which they stood. "You with the Mannlicher right here. You can hit anyone on the radio station's road, and if any of them make a break for town, hit them in the back."

He turned to Gadgets. "A quick booby trap on the gate—"

"A phosphorous grenade—"

"The gate's closed, they stop to open it, boom. The shooting starts. Lyons, let me take your Ingram. Let's go."

In two minutes they had set the ambush, Lyons on the ridge, Blancanales lower on the hillside, only a hundred feet from the road opposite him. Gadgets closed the gate. He pulled the pin from a white phosphorous grenade and placed it carefully on one of the gate's hinges, using the gate to hold the lever closed.

Lyons heard motorcycles. He whistled a warning. Gadgets sprinted through the brush and threw himself flat a few yards from Blancanales.

Chief had reached the gate already, and he waited for the stragglers to join him, his bike drawn up parallel to the gate. He carried an M-60 machine gun slung over his back like a rifle. In his Italian wraparound shades and Mohawk haircut, the road's dust swirling around him, he looked like a demon from hell.

Lyons watched him through the Mannlicher's scope, the biker's face and chest filling the image. Chief turned from side to side, counting his men.

Panning back and forth across the bikers, Lyons suddenly noted a hideous ornament on the forks of

Chief's bike. The head of a man, the eyes wide and staring, had been wired to the handlebars.

"Ready to die, freak show?" Lyons whispered, his finger on the Mannlicher's trigger.

Chief kicked the gate open, then gunned his bike. Gadgets saw the grenade drop. But Chief accelerated away. In the six seconds before the grenade exploded, Chief would ride to safety. Gadgets sighted his Uzi on Chief. He fired. The biker spilled splashily.

All the bikers, the two pulling off the highway, the several near the gate, the others gunning their motorcycles up the road, turned their heads fast toward the Uzi-fire. The distraction served only to make them less ready for what followed. An exploding ball of white flame engulfed the road.

Five human forms were directly hit. Hundreds of droplets of white phosphorous splattered their bodies, each drop a searing point of flame that burned through cloth and leather and flesh. Not requiring oxygen to burn, the metallic fire would continue through their flesh to the bone and burn there until the metal consumed itself. But they died before that agony. Their motorcycles' gasoline was exploding. Screaming, the bikers inhaled gulps of fire into their lungs, died in seconds.

Dust and flame and smoke filled the scope's image, but Lyons still squeezed off a shot at the downed Chief. Then he opened his left eye, searching the road for targets, his right eye still at the eyepiece.

Automatic fire from Gadgets and Blancanales poured into the two bikers immediately behind the fallen Chief. The hillside beyond the bikers puffed into a sheet of dust as slugs punched through the two men. Other bullets tore through the sheet metal of the gas tanks.

Seeing the annihilation of the patrol, the last two Outlaws spun their motorcycles, throwing dust and rocks as their rear wheels skittered on the dirt road. Lyons put the Mannlicher's cross hairs in the center of the "Outlaws Forever" insignia on a biker's jacket. His shot snapped the man's spine.

Whipping back the bolt, Carl Lyons put the next slug into the second biker's head.

On the road, a biker lay under his motorcycle. Through the scope, Lyons saw blood streaming from wounds in Chief's head and chest. One arm flopped, broken a few inches below the shoulder. He struggled against the weight of the motorcycle with one arm. He was trying to reach for the belt-fed M-60. Lyons put the cross hairs on the man's forehead. But he didn't shoot.

He jerked back the bolt, caught the unfired Accelerator. Searching through the pouches of his bandolier, he found the .308 tracers. Lyons loaded up, then snapped the tracer through the struggling biker's gas tank. Immediately a churning ball of flame rose above Chief. His screams continued for thirty seconds.

Then there was silence.

"Lyons!" Blancanales shouted. "You see anything moving?"

Motorcycle tires burned, filling the narrow canyon mouth with acrid rubber smoke. Around the gate, a brushfire spread up the slope. By the time he had gazed over the blackened scene of bone and scorched flesh, Lyons could see nothing that was living. He searched the rock and brush of the stream-bed.

He saw the barrel of an M-60. The muzzle flashed. Lyons flew backward, his body exploding with pain.

Streams of .308 slugs suddenly shrieking over them, Gadgets and Blancanales sprayed back with 9mm Parabellum. The machinegunner fell behind his rock for an instant, then popped out a few yards away, still firing his belt-fed M-60.

Slugs marched across the hillside, chopping brush, making the earth around Blancanales jump. "Lyons!" Blancanales screamed. "Hit him, hit him!"

There was no rifle fire, no answer from the ridge.

Burst after burst searched for Blancanales. Desperate, he screamed again, but this time without words, his voice shuddering with faked agony. He screamed until his throat ached, then let his wail die to a whimper. "Arm...my arm...it's...off." After a second, he wailed again. "My arm—oh God oh God oh God...."

"Rosario!" Gadgets cried.

Another long burst searched for Gadgets. He rolled clear, crawled toward Blancanales. Hissed words stopped him:

"Lay cool! I'm all right, see? It's Lyons up there we got to worry about. Radio!"

Keying his hand-radio, Gadgets got no reply. "Lyons! Answer. Answer! Lyons...."

No reply.

Gadgets crawled back to Blancanales. "We got to bring this show to a close."

"Frag him? Or phosphorous?"

"We need that M-60 of his."

"Frags." Blancanales took a fragmentation grenade from the battle rig under his Outlaws jacket. He straightened the cotter pin, saying: "Wanted to save these for tonight, when we—"

"There won't be any tonight for us if we don't use them now." Gadgets braced himself to throw. "On three. Yours to the right, mine on the left. Pull. Now, one and two and three!"

The surviving biker, dizzy from blood loss, saw the arms heave the grenades. He snapped a burst at the hidden men as the grenades arced toward him. One grenade hit a rock and bounced over him. The other landed exactly three feet in front of him.

He snatched up the grenade and threw it back. He struggled to crawl a few feet, the exposed bones of his right leg scraping on rocks, the pain beyond imagination.

Then an explosion of thousands of steel razors shredded his legs and punched tiny holes in the back of his head. The rush of even greater pain lifted him into darkness. The grenade he had thrown had exploded in midair, and fragments of steel wire were showering even Gadgets and Blancanales.

The grenade sent tiny slivers into their backs. Blancanales felt blood on his hands. He looked at his hands and saw bits of wire in the flesh. Gadgets had tiny cuts also.

The wounds did not stop them. They fired into their target's twisted, mangled body, the bursts of 9mm slugs throwing him over. Gadgets put a burst into the guy's haircut, spraying it and everything else rosily over the creek bed.

"Think he's dead?" Blancanales joked.

"Might be. Let's go make sure."

Breaking cover, they zigzagged down the hillside. They crouched beside the biker's almost headless body.

"Take the M-60, I'll check his bike for belts of .308." Blancanales ran up the embankment to a big downed Suzuki. He searched through the saddlebags and found two belts of two hundred and fifty .308 cartridges. He slung them around his shoulders, then slid back down to the creek bed.

He heard motorcycles. "Gadgets. They're coming."

They looked up the hillside for cover. Too far. They saw the culvert. They glanced to each other, and without a word ran through the rocks and sand mounds to the shelter of the highway's overhang. Above them, motorcycles screeched to a stop.

"Oh, sweet Jesus!" a voice cried. "Someone's out here with a flame thrower."

"Chief!" another biker called out. "Chief, where are you?"

Shotgun blasts chopped brush, kicked up dust on the hillside opposite the ambush site. The casings clattered on the rocks in front of Gadgets and Blancanales. They heard four or five or six more motorcycles arrive.

"It's all over here," a voice announced. "Look at them all, all burned to death." More shotgun blasts of frustration peppered the hillside.

Gadgets pulled the third phosphorous grenade from his battle rig. He whispered to Blancanales. "My last one."

"Make it a good throw. No bounce back."

Gadgets jerked the pin, held down the lever.

He took three steps, then turned and looked up at the gathered bikers.

"Hi guys," he said. Then he lobbed up the white phosphorous, jumped the hell back to cover.

"Kick it!!"

White molten metal showered the creek bed. There was screaming. Falling bikes. Exploding gas tanks. The conflagration, and the cries of agony, continued noisily for quite some time. A lot of smoke. A lot of smell. A lot of slow, sure death.

Blancanales had his hand-radio to his mouth. "Lyons, come in. Lyons! Lyons!"

No answer.

12

In the Casino's ballroom, the hostages' prison, Max
Stevens had organized a cadre of resisters. Persuading, explaining, sometimes preaching, he turned angry
islanders into leaders, fearful residents into spies.

"I've got to do something," a father told Max and
the group of conspirators. "When they dragged that
last girl out, they looked at my daughters and said,
'We'll be back for them.' In the name of God,
they're only twelve and fourteen years old! I'm going
to grab one of their guns, I don't care what happens,
they won't take my girls."

Max spoke calmly, slowly. "Since we circled up,
they haven't taken another girl, have they?" After
the Outlaws had stalked through the crowd of hostages several times, each time dragging away teenage
girls, Max had suggested the hostages form a tight
circle, men and women and teenage boys on the outside, children and teenage girls inside. Later, when
two Outlaws came in, they saw an unbroken wall of
men and women facing them. They had turned and
left.

"When do we hit them?" another father asked.
"They hurt my girl every way there is. It's us against
them. If the police were coming, they'd be here already."

"That's not true!" Max explained. "If there's a ransom to be paid, remember it's Sunday. The police will have to open banks. If they're negotiating for something, that could take days. SWAT teams could hit those scum any second now, or tonight, or tomorrow. If we fight at the wrong time, the police will bust in here and only find dead people.

"If we hit at the right time, we're helping the police. We'll hit those creatures when we hear shooting—we'll shoot them, knife them, take their weapons.

"I promise you, the police won't get a chance to take any Outlaws prisoner. Prisoners sell their memoirs to publishers, make movie deals. No, we have to wait, but when we hit, they all die."

"Does that mean we wait a year?" the red-eyed parent demanded. "How about four hundred and forty-four days? I'd rather die."

"It won't be long," Max told the man, then spoke to the others. "Things are happening outside. People are fighting. Shirley, tell them what you've learned."

A middle-aged woman in a jogging suit spoke. "Whenever I see one of them with a walkie-talkie, I get one of my people to go up to the creep and ask for something—food, water, medicine, magazines, anything. Two of my spies heard the bikers yelling at their radios about heroes, kill them, make an example. One time when I went up, I heard, 'His rifle's gone, the ammunition too.' That's a word for word quote. The punk got real agitated, punched me, but it was worth it." She touched her blackening eye.

"They're all getting agitated," another man said. "They're not so cocky. Something's got them scared."

A tourist came up to Shirley. He was a middle-aged man in a suit. Gray hair streaked his temples. "Can I talk to your leader?"

"Leader?" she asked, confused. "Leader of what? Who do you mean?"

"I'm Mike Carst." The stately tourist shook hands with her. "Of the RayShine Corporation. Who is the man who limps?"

"You mean Max?" She didn't really trust the tourists. The group had decided not to involve non-residents in their planning and organization. The tourists had no stake in the community: they would not weigh the value of their lives against the lives of the island's families; to save themselves, they might betray the island people; or a tourist might even be an Outlaw spy.

"He must be the mayor, correct?" Mike Carst continued.

"No, he sells houses. He has a number of ice cream accounts too."

"He appears very military."

"His wife told me he used to be a sergeant in the army. He was in a war and he got hurt. He's lived here ever since. Knows everybody. But he's not a leader of anything. He's just talking to people, keeping them calm."

"I'd like to talk to him. It's very important."

"I don't think an appointment is necessary," Shirley said.

Max was limping up to them. Max recognized the stranger as one of the men guarded by the murdered Secret Service agent.

"Mike Carst, sir." The stranger shook hands with Max. "And your name?"

"Max. You don't live on the island, do you?"

"No, Max. I'm only a visitor."

"Mr. Carst thinks you're some kind of leader," Shirley told Max.

"A leader? Me?"

Carst took Max's arm, led him away from Shirley to an open area where they wouldn't be overheard. "Putting the charade aside, I have information for you and your people. In turn, I need your help."

"What is the information?"

"One of the men in my party has a radio. He appears to be communicating at hourly intervals with someone outside. If you have your people watch this man...if they could possibly overhear a transmission—both our groups would benefit. Do we have an agreement?"

"Why are you and the Secret Service on the island?" Max asked.

"Secret Service?" Carst smiled.

"Agreed, then," Max told him. "From now on, you don't talk to me. You must point the man out to Shirley. She'll organize the surveillance. A pleasure doing business with you. Goodbye."

Max moved on to the Websters, Jack's parents. Mr. Webster grabbed Max by the arm. His voice quavered: "Jack here, he's just told us something. He's not a bad kid, really. He's troubled, but...."

"What is it, Webster?" glared Max.

"They're going to tear him apart limb from limb, they're going to castrate him for God's sake, up on that stage over there unless he spies for them. Unless he tells them everything that's going on in here, everything we've planned. He just told us. It's not the kid's fault—''

Max interrupted. ''Don't sweat it. Relax. So he'll do exactly what they told him to do.'' He turned to the stricken youth. ''Jack will give them all sorts of information, won't you, lad? You're going to feed them everything we want them to hear.''

Climbing up the thick trunk of the carob tree, Glen Shepard walked along a branch. He stepped off of it onto the roof of the house. He pushed through the leaves and branches that shaded the roof. He stood at the rear of the house, concealed by the lush foliage. He was armed with his Colt, and he wore a biker's jacket. Between him and the front of the house, there was thirty feet of open roof.

Smoke billowed at the far end of the block. From where he stood, he saw only the smoke. He heard shouts, a few shots. But to observe the Outlaws, he would have to cross the open roof to where his view was unobstructed.

To his left, the direction of the Outlaws, there was no cover. To his right, a neighbor's row of tall cedars screened that side. He had to chance it.

He crawled to that side of the roof ridge. Motorcycles passed. He froze, waited until the motorcycles stopped at the far end of the block, then he continued. Any Outlaw who happened to glance up to the roof could see him. He hurried to the front, then looked.

At the end of the block, the two-story house in

which they had hidden was burning. Outlaws watched the house, shotguns and assault rifles ready. Carrying red and yellow cans of gasoline, other Outlaws ran to the next house.

Glen crabbed back to the tree and thrashed through the branches. He scampered along the branch until it merged with the trunk, then hopped the last six feet and started for the back door.

"Hey, brother. See any of those hero locos?"

Reaching for the Magnum under his leather jacket, Glen turned. A Latin-featured Outlaw with a Fu Man-chu mustache and a chromed Nazi helmet lounged in the yard, an M-14 rifle cradled in his hands. Seeing Glen's face, the biker realized his mistake. He brought up the rifle. Glen jerked the Colt Lawman from his belt.

The revolver's hammer snagged on Glen's shirt. Even before he heard the shot, he knew he was about to die.

His head exploding, the biker flew aside, his dead finger sending a burst into the carob's trunk and the next-door house. Window glass fell. Glen disentangled the Colt from his shirt, pointed the Magnum everywhere in the yard, looking for any other bikers. Shooting continued elsewhere in the neighborhood. Glen went to the back door, looked inside the house.

Chris Davis gagged, the auto-loading shotgun on the floor beside him. Glen jerked him to his feet, put the shotgun in his hands.

"Great timing, kid. But get sick later, I need you to cover the driveway."

Wiping his mouth, Chris nodded. He lifted the auto-loader and went to a window over the driveway.

Glen dashed outside, stripped the biker's jacket, weapons and ammunition. He had no radio. Seeing the helmet, Glen spilled out the blood and took possession of it also.

"Stay here," Glen told Chris. He dropped the jacket and helmet beside the teenager. "Put those on." Then he ran into the living room, where his wife and Roger watched the street.

"We couldn't warn you!" Ann told him.

"Chris took care of him. Pack up, we're moving again."

"What's going on up there?" Roger asked.

"They're burning the block. We've got to find someplace to hide where they won't look, won't even suspect—"

"Where?" Ann asked.

"I don't know," he told them. "I don't know."

Running up the hillside, Blancanales saw Carl's body sprawled just below the ridge. "Oh, no! Lyons, Lyons."

Blancanales ripped the compact first-aid kit from his battle rig, and popped open the plastic lid as he fell to his knees beside Lyons. Something sagged under the bullet-torn Outlaws jacket. Hoping to God he wouldn't see spilled intestines, Blancanales opened the jacket.

The .308 slug had sliced across Lyons' ribs, cutting the nylon strap of the bandolier of cartridges for the Mannlicher. It was the bandolier that made the bulge in the jacket. Blancanales tore open Lyons' shirt, looking for the wound. A long, bloody gash marked the path of the slug. But only at one small point did the white of a rib show. There were no other bullet wounds. Lyons groaned.

"Ah, you crazy bastard, you're alive!" Blancanales half-lifted his friend from the dirt and dry grass of the slope.

"Let me go, Latin lover," Lyons groaned. "Oh...does my head hurt."

Blancanales took a squeeze bottle of alcohol from his kit and doused the long wound as Lyons lay back. The ex-cop jerked up, his eyes wide with pain. He shoved the squeeze bottle away, then touched the back of his head, his hand coming away bloody.

They both glanced up the hillside and saw one particular rock. Some of Lyons' hair and blood smeared the jutting stone. "What luck," Lyons griped. "One rock on the hill, and I hit my head on it."

"Don't knock your luck. It's not every day you get machine-gunned and walk away from it." He finished his fast job of local bandaging.

"I'm not walking anywhere, I hurt. Do I hurt...."

The older man jerked Lyons to his feet. He handed him the Mannlicher and bandolier of cartridges. "March or die, Lyons. The cavalry's on the way, and we're the Indians."

They returned slowly to the ridge to where they had left their motorcycles. Blancanales radioed ahead: "Good news, Gadgets. There's three of us yet."

Lyons looked back at the ambush. Tires were still burning. Charred bodies littered the highway and road. He counted corpses.

"Sixteen. Decent score."

Already at the motorcycles, Gadgets lashed the black plastic-wrapped M-60 to his bike's chromed roll bar. As he saw Blancanales and Lyons approaching, he told them: "We got a new development."

He switched on the scanner/auto-recorder's play back: "This is Brognola, Stony Man Farm. I have received information from a joint FBI/CIA investigation. Details suggest one of the theoreticians may be a Soviet agent planted in American atomic energy program back in the late fifties. Repeat, Soviet long-term agent, a mole. Investigation is ongoing.

"There is not yet conclusive evidence that he is in fact an enemy agent," the familiar voice continued, undetected by the Outlaws because of scrambling. "However, on his return from the West Coast, he was to be transferred to a non-military study group. His name is John Severine. His photo, description, and biographical details are in the folder on the theoreticians. We attempted to match the voice you recorded to his lecture tapes. However, it is not possible to conclusively confirm or eliminate Severine is the voice due to electronic degradation of voice as received. Request brief broadcast of voice without scrambler or screech. Voicegraph then possible.

"FBI/CIA investigators urge capture of Severine. It is imperative he does not escape.

"Presence of Severine on the island, and his possible complicity in seizure, precludes fulfillment of one point in ransom demands. By highest authority, under no circumstances will nuclear submarine make delivery of the released felons and twenty million dollars in gold. Diesel submarine will make delivery. Severine is very knowledgeable of nuclear submarines. He can be expected to recognize the substitution, and this may affect fate of hostages. Highest authority accepts responsibility.

"Coordinated assault impossible while gang surrounds hostages. LAPD units are on standby, full alert. You disperse Outlaws, then call for units. Also, Outlaw radio conversations have been monitored by private craft beyond three-mile limit. Media are now aware of crisis. *Please resolve at earliest possible time.* Out." The emphasis was clear.

"A Soviet agent teamed up with a bike gang?" Lyons shook his head. "Far out. Only in California," he added, gazing over the hills. The three men stood in the early afternoon sun, refueling their confidence for the higher stakes yet to come. They were battle weary, battle sore, that was the truth.

13

Her hands up in the air, the shotgun against her back, Ann Shepard stepped off the curb. She stumbled slightly. Roger caught her arm with his good hand. The Outlaw behind him cruelly jabbed him with the barrel of an M-14 rifle, sending the curly-haired teenager sprawling in the street. Roger grimaced with pain as he fell on his rag-wrapped right arm. Blood stained the cloth. The Outlaws stood over him, their weapons pointed at him, until he stood and walked again.

The Outlaws, one in a chromed Nazi helmet, the other sporting a bandage on his face and a stubble of beard, pushed the teenager and pregnant woman across the shady street. In addition to the weapons that the bikers pointed at Ann and Roger, they carried shotguns slung over their backs. They wore pistol belts. Bandoliers crossed their jacket's insignia of flaming skull: "Forever Outlaws."

A block behind them, several houses smoked and crackled. Outlaws stood on the sidewalk, assault rifles and shotguns ready. They could care less if the entire island ignited into flame. From time to time, they fired at a movement or shadow in the side yards. They had contingency plans for major fire. They thought they had contingency plans for everything.

As fast as the pregnant woman could walk, the Outlaws marched their prisoners the length of the block, leaving Avalon's residential area. At Crescent Street, the Outlaws prodded them down toward the Casino.

Tourists usually crowded Crescent on Sundays. Only steps from the sand, its shops and hotels viewed the boats moored in Avalon Bay. But today, the warm wind stirring the palms carried smoke and ash. Today, broken plate glass and litter from the looted shops covered the deserted street and walkways.

The Outlaws on motorcycles cruised past the bikers escorting the prisoners; they slowed. Not looking-back as the Outlaws U-turned, the biker with his face bandaged shoved the pregnant woman:

"The hotel!"

They herded their prisoners through the doorway. A few steps behind the bikers, the Outlaws on motorcycles jumped the curb, stepped on their kickstands and dismounted.

"It's a party!"

"Forget that. Any woman with a belly that big's only good for head."

"Take what you want," the Outlaw laughed, "and I'll take mine."

Only seconds behind their buddies, they walked into the hotel's lobby. But there was no one there. They heard feet running up the stairs.

"Hey, us too!" The Outlaws ran up the stairs after the others.

The fire door to the second floor slowly swung closed. They whipped it open and saw Outlaw jackets enter one of the rooms. Laughing, they ran after the other bikers. One of the Outlaws called out, "Second on her!" The other laughed, shouted, "First on the boy!"

Pushing open the door, they saw the curly-haired teenager, the pregnant woman, and the Outlaw in the chromed helmet all pointing weapons at them.

As the two Outlaws stumbled astounded back, a hidden hand put a Colt Lawman to the head of the second Outlaw, spraying his brains onto the hotel room's wall. The other Outlaw fell backwards over the body, tried to crawl, looked up to see the Colt and a 12-gauge muzzle pointing at his face. He rolled onto his back and put his hands up, pleaded: "I give up, you got me, please don't please don't don't—"

The Colt's flash slammed his head back. Glen Shepard dragged the messy bodies into the room and closed the door. He stripped off the dead men's jackets, no filthier for all the new gore than they were before. He threw the larger to his wife, the smaller to Roger.

"Welcome to the Outlaws."

In the ballroom's crowd of hostages, Max Stevens and Mr. Webster rehearsed Jack for his report to Horse:

"What are the people doing?" Max demanded.

"They're just trying to protect the girls. They figured that if they circled up, your bikers wouldn't risk a fight with a hundred people at once."

"Did you see any guns?"

"You have guns? Wow—"

The shove sent Jack reeling. Max stepped forward and shook the teenager, then drew back his fist. "You didn't answer my question! Tell me!"

"Don't hit my boy!" Jack's father grabbed Max, trying to break his grip. Max shrugged the overweight, middle-aged man away.

"What do you think's going to happen when he goes to talk with that psychopath?" Max asked Mr. Webster. Then he shook Jack again: "Tell me what you saw."

"They don't have anything. They're just a bunch of dumb people."

Speaking gently, Max told Jack: "That's not what you want to say. Say, 'They're just a bunch of dumb people. Some of them are talking about escape, but they're too scared.' Now repeat that."

Jack repeated the line. Max released the kid, took his father aside. "If he doesn't say something like that, then they don't need a spy anymore. They caught him with a rifle. They think he shot at their gang. Your son's only alive because they need a spy. I'm sorry to abuse him, but I'm just trying to keep him alive."

Max returned his attention to Jack and resumed the rehearsal. The teenager repeated his lines time after time, almost perfectly. Finally Max glanced at his watch:

"It's time, Jack. It would be better if you went to them, like a loyal agent, instead of making them find you. You should say goodbye to your father and mother now."

"Tell Mr. Stevens thank you, son," Mr. Webster prompted. "He's probably saved your life."

"Yeah," Jack said. "Thanks a whole lot."

Jack turned his back so that he could speak alone with his parents. "Any chance for an escape soon?"

he asked in a whisper. "How much longer before we rush the bikers and break out?"

"I'm sure Max will tell us about that when you get back," Mr. Webster said.

"But we will break out, right? I mean, we won't be like this for days and days."

"Mr. Stevens is a godsend, Jack." Mrs. Webster ran her hands through her son's permed blond hair. "Without him, we'd have no hope at all."

"Yeah." Jack watched Max Stevens limp through the crowd, stopping to encourage the fearful, to comfort the despairing citizens of the island. "He's a real hero."

Horse stared out at Avalon Bay and the ocean beyond. He stood with Jack Webster on the balcony that encircled the Casino. The doors behind them led to the ballroom and the wide flights of stairs descending to the mezzanine, the theater, and the museum that was once the gambling salon.

After the seizure of the town, Horse had placed his heavy weapons—the Browning .50 caliber machine guns, the LAAW rockets, the mortars and the .444 Marlin sniper rifles—on this balcony. Any assault unit attempting to rescue the hostages, whether they came by sea or land, would face fire directed at them from one hundred and fifty feet above the street. And if the attackers returned the fire, they would hit the hostages.

A squad of Outlaws had secured the hill inland of the Casino. Even if rescuers took that hill, they would gain nothing. Hundreds of feet of open air separated the hill from the Casino. Unless the attackers had wings, they could only snipe at the Outlaws. The morfars would annihilate the attackers in a minute.

"—they circled up the people because your guys kept taking girls. They figured your bikers wouldn't want to fight a hundred people at once."

Horse looked to Charlie. "Sheep tactics. Next time someone wants a piece of ass, take an Uzi in there. See how brave those people are after ten or twenty get blown away. Go on, keep talking," he spat at Jack. "What about guns and knives? What do they have?"

"I didn't see anything. But I think they do. Everybody's talking about escaping. How they'd get past the guards and so on. But they haven't let me in on their plans yet. Maybe later."

"They're working on an escape, huh?"

"Everyone's talking about it."

"Who's everybody?"

"All the people in there—"

"Who's talking the most? Who's going to lead the escape?"

"I can find out."

"Get me names, boy."

Smoke obscured Avalon. The afternoon winds, sweeping down from the canyons, fanned the burning homes. Even from where Able Team watched on the Divide Road, two miles from Avalon Bay, the flames could be seen, from time to time lighting the underside of the smoke clouds or leaping up high, the tongues of flame for an instant defeating the afternoon brilliance.

Sharing the binoculars and the Mannlicher's scope, Blancanales, Gadgets and Lyons studied the burning neighborhood. Though trees and smoke allowed them only snatches of vision, they saw the Outlaws pacing the block, cruising around the block on their motorcycles. Only one group of houses burned. And it was those that the Outlaws circled.

The voices on the Outlaws' walkie-talkie, recorded by Schwarz, explained what Able Team watched: "We were standing in front of the house. It burned. They couldn't have got out." "Hey, tell that to Zapata. While you're watching the fire, he walked into them and they blew his head off. Clean off. Had to look at his boots to figure out who he was." "They must've got away before we burned that one house. Now they're dead, because we burned them all. The whole block's gone. Nothing but crispy critters in there now." "Want to bet they weren't even *in* those houses? Bet they split long time—"

"This is Horse. Shut up! Has anyone out there seen the Monk? His patrol went to help the Chief. Has anyone seen him? Anyone heard a radio call from him?"

"This is Stonewall. I'll go out and find the Chief and the Monk and all their men. Give me the word, Horse, I'll be on—" "No! Stonewall, everyone else—no one leaves the town. No one! Like the Chief said, the locals out there know the territory. We're not losing one more brother to those crazies. Come tonight, we're rich men. We'll be in another country living like kings! So everyone hang tight. We hold the town. Twenty million in gold, remember that."

"Forget your plan, you low-life," Lyons muttered. "Tonight you die."

Blancanales glanced at his watch, looked at the sun. "We've got four hours until dusk. We need to circle around the town, check out the Outlaws' perimeter, find their outposts and sentries—"

"These bikers are such losers," Lyons said. "If they've even got outposts around the town, I'll be surprised."

Gadgets grinned. He wore colored spectacles to diffuse the bright coastal daylight. "Surprised? Like that biker with the M-60 surprised you? We meet up with two or three of *him* at an outpost, Stony Man will be running want ads for another Able Team."

Lyons touched the wound across his ribs. "Ooo ah... I am self-criticized!"

"Hurt much?" Blancanales asked.

"Yeah."

"The numbing from shock is wearing off. That rib isn't broken but I'd say all the cartilage between your ribs on that side is separated. Like shatter lines in glass. But you played football—it'll feel like a blindside elbow attack, except ten times worse. I have some painkillers."

"Forget the dope."

"Carl, you're going to hurt."

"I'll get through it. What good will I be if I'm doped up? The pain will motivate me to close down this horror show. Let's go find those outposts."

Descending the mountain's firebreaks and trails on their captured motorcycles, Lyons fell back, unable to keep up with Blancanales and Gadgets. Every bump, every lurch of the handlebars made his face go tight with pain. A few hundred yards short of the highway, Gadgets pulled behind a screen of manzanita and sage where they could not possibly be seen. He raised his hand to stop the others.

"Change in plans. If Lyons can't keep up on a motorcycle, how's he going to do it when we're running and jumping and crawling?"

"I can do it," Lyons insisted, his face tight. Despite the exertion of the motocrossing, he tried to hold his upper body motionless, taking shallow breaths.

"Lyons, you are hard core. But you're also walking wounded. What do you two say we just ride our bikes down the highway and cruise through town? Make like bikers on patrol?"

Now Lyons was smiling. "Taking a long chance, wizard."

"Like you said, they're losers. A gang of psycho losers. I think we can slip in and slip out—"

"With luck," Blancanales nodded. "But we'll need helmets. I want to cover these, too." He glanced down at the black nylon of his battle-suit's pants. He unfolded his map and pointed out the dotted line of a fire road. "This becomes a paved road a mile out of town. It comes down to that block that's burning. In all the smoke, maybe we could get what we need. Without any trouble. Maybe...." Blancanales held his silenced Beretta to chamber a round.

They followed Stage Road only a quarter mile, then turned off onto the Indian Trail service road. The heavy motorcycles were able to follow the twisting trail, powerfully, and they climbed the steep hills with gusts of noisy energy.

At the Country Club, the fire road became a paved, gently graded asphalt lane lined by rows of eucalyptus trees. Bougainvillea and oleander bloomed on the roadside.

They switched off their engines and coasted through the cool afternoon shadows. Only the whirring of their spoked wheels would betray them.

Soon, smoke obscured the sky. Only a few hundred yards farther on, homes were burning. The sound of shotgun blasts stopped them. Pulling over, Blancanales and Gadgets hotfooted it around a turn in the road, leaving Lyons with the motorcycles.

Two Outlaws braced their weapons on the bricks of a low wall, firing at a man running across a horse pasture. Despite several blasts from a shotgun and a burst from an M-16, the man continued running. Only another hundred yards remained between him and the safety of the brush-covered hillsides. The Outlaw with the M-16 dropped out the magazine, fumbled to insert another. He saw Gadgets and Blancanales approaching. He wore aviator-style sunglasses.

"We flushed a Mexican out of the stables," he grunted. "Get with it and put out some firepower. That funky little beaner ain't gonna get away."

Blancanales brought up the Beretta. "Yes he is."

14

As Roger Davis watched Crescent Street for Outlaws, Glen Shepard and Chris Davis wheeled the motorcycles of the recently deceased bikers into the hotel. They continued with the bikes through the hotel to the linen storage and sorting room. They hid the motorcycles under dirty towels and sheets, then went back to the lobby.

"You know how to ride one of those things?" Glen asked Chris.

"Oh, yeah. Roger has a Honda dirt-bike. You think we could just ride out to the hills? Hide out up there?"

"Only if you teach me how."

"We could get a car."

Glen called to Roger. The young man left the front door and followed Glen and his cousin up the stairs. "You two want to go into the hills until this is over?"

"Whatever you think is safe, Mr. Shepard," Roger answered.

"No, it's not what I think. It's what we think. You stay here, you're in danger. You try to make it to the hills, you're in danger. If you two got on those Harleys, you could be in the hills in two or three minutes. My wife and I, we'd have to get a car. And I don't think driving through town in a car would be smart."

"You've done great so far," Roger assured him.

"We've done great so far," Glen corrected him. "Without you two—in the attic and in that backyard—Ann and I wouldn't be around anymore. It's just that everywhere I hide, they find me."

They laughed, almost relaxed. In the hotel room, Ann sat at the window watching the street. Below, the cough and roar of motorcycles passed by, then faded as they continued along the Bay.

"Those Outlaws just then," Ann told them. "They were nervous, watching all the streets, the doorways. Like they expected to get shot at."

"They see you?" Glen asked. He went to the window and looked to the south. Three bikers had passed the ferry boat docks and were heading toward the southern end of the island.

"No, they didn't see me. They didn't even look up. They were too busy looking left and right. What do we do now?"

"You want to go to the hills? Or you want to stay here? The boys could take those motorcycles, but we'd have to chance a car."

"And that means we'd have to chance driving through the Outlaws. And that means we'd have to chance a gunfight, right? Forget it. I want to go to sleep. I mean I feel like a zombie. I don't have any iron in my blood and all night I've been chased around by psychopaths. The doctor told me to rest, to stay in bed until the baby is born. We're safe enough here. This'll all be over pretty soon—"

"And if it isn't?" Glen asked.

"If it's still going on tomorrow, if the police haven't come, then we'll talk about the hills. Now, I want to sleep. Find me a safe place to sleep and I'll be a very happy woman.''

"Okay, we stay. Ann and I. What about you two?"

Chris looked to Roger. "I'll stay here if—"

"Sure," Roger said. "But what do we do if the Outlaws look for us?"

"This hotel has three floors. We're higher than most of the other places on Crescent. We could block the stairwells and jam the elevator. If they tried to burn the hotel, we could drop down on the roof of the restaurant and make a run for it."

"Sure, Glen," Ann said. "I'm going to run over the rooftops. Come up with another plan."

"Well, any Outlaw who tries to come up the stairs, we kill. If they try to burn the hotel, we shoot them. We'll be up on the roof. We'll have the advantage."

"And we've got guns just like they do," Chris added. "We won't surrender like those two old people. We could hit anything on the street. Be snipers."

Motorcycles passed on the street again. Automatically, they reached for their weapons. Shotgun in hand, Glen looked at the teenagers and saw how their hands closed around the M-14 and the autoloading shotgun.

"Maybe tonight, maybe tomorrow. Everything in a leather jacket dies."

Smoke blew about them and flame-light flashed from their sunglasses. The three Outlaws low-geared through the devastated neighborhood. They saw black skeletal trees, fire-gutted cars, the ruins of homes. Other homes still smoldered, walls collapsing as the Outlaws passed.

The three-man patrol wore the Outlaw uniform: black jackets, old jeans, boots, helmets, weapons. Unlike the other Outlaws on the street, the three-man patrol all wore soft leather combat boots. None of the Outlaws splashing gasoline or watching the burning homes saw the boots. They saw only the motorcycles, the uniforms, the weapons, the skull and flame insignias.

Leaving the burning block, the patrol cruised through a neighborhood of bullet-pocked, looted homes. Turning south on Crescent Street, they continued their survey of the town, scrutinizing smashed windows of shops and hotels, the walkways strewn with new clothing, broken liquor bottles, window displays. They could see the body of a Deputy Sheriff bobbing in the small waves under Pleasure Pier. They saw two motorcycles parked at the door to the Harbor master's office. They passed other Outlaws on motorcycles. But scanning the windows and roof lines, they saw no Outlaw sentry positions.

Two blocks south of the pier, they returned to the residential blocks. They watched the hillsides above the neighborhoods and still saw no outposts.

"Maybe they have snipers hidden up there," Lyons said.

Blancanales probed with his eyes the heavy brush that covered the hills. "Everywhere the Outlaws go, their bikes go. Up there, it's too steep for a motorcycle. The brush is too thick."

"They were smart enough to seize the island," Gadgets said. "They have to be smart enough to know about sentries and outposts."

"All we've seen are patrols," Blancanales reminded him.

"So far," Gadgets said, steering off into the street.

Passing the burning block again, they continued their circuit of the town. Coming to Crescent once more, they turned north toward the Casino, but quickly turned again onto Vieudelou Street. Vieudelou took them into a more expensive area. Higher in the hills, the homes viewed the town and Bay and the San Pedro Channel beyond. When Vieudelou ended at Stage Road, they stopped to consult the map.

"Town's wide open," Lyons commented. "Except for patrols. No wonder they've had problems with the locals. Avoid the patrols, you've got the run of the streets."

"Uh huh," Blancanales unfolded a map. "Why don't you just go walking down those streets in your blacksuit, no jacket, no motorcycle. We'll see if you draw fire."

Blancanales pointed out another dotted line on the map. "That's a firebreak and hiking trail. It passes behind the Casino. Instead of pushing our luck, how about checking out the place from a distance?"

The others nodded. They continued north on Stage Road for less than a mile and came to the trail. The fire road followed the crest of the steep hills overlooking Avalon. Beyond Avalon, the vista continued to Los Angeles, twenty-two miles distant.

Gunning their machines up the steep inclines, gearing and braking to slow their descent of the ridges, they watched for the tracks of other motorcycles. Surprisingly they saw only the knobby prints of lightweight dirt bikes. Blancanales stopped briefly to examine these tracks.

"Yesterday. Local kids."

The next peak, things were different. It was the Outlaw outpost guarding the hill above the Casino. Lyons had accelerated to climb the hill, and when he shot over the crest, he had to swerve to avoid the Harleys and Nighthawks of four Outlaws.

Sitting against their bikes, the Outlaws passed a joint. One Outlaw spoke into a walkie-talkie. Lyons hurtled past them, then hit his brakes. He slid to a stop thirty feet past the group. His body blocked their view of the Ingram in his grip. Below him, not far off, Lyons saw the Casino. Outlaws lounged in front of the white building, servicing their motorcycles and drinking. They were so close Lyons heard their voices and laughter.

"Looking for locals," Lyons shouted, hoping his voice would warn Gadgets and Blancanales. Even as he called out, Blancanales, then Gadgets leaped over the hill on their machines. Flashing the Outlaws quick glances, they slowed, but Lyons waved both of his partners past him. They roared on, and he accelerated after them.

The trail cut sharply to the south. Once down there, the Outlaws back on the peak could not see them. Close shave. Able Team had not expected that outpost: no tracks, at least not where they had looked.

"I couldn't chance wasting them," Lyons told his teammates, their bikes idling.

Gadgets pulled the captured walkie-talkie from his pocket and listened. "...up on the hill. Just now, not even a minute ago, we had a patrol swing by. I didn't recognize the three guys. Did you send anyone by this way?" "I've got lots of patrols out. I'll call

them. This is Horse. Patrol on the ridgeline behind
the Casino, report. On the ridgeline behind the
Casino, report...."

Gadgets offered the walkie-talkie to Blancanales,
then Lyons. "That's us. Want to report to Horse?"

"We only got a minute," Lyons told Blancanales.
"Look what he's got on the balcony down there.
Looks like .50 calibers."

"Sentries on all the doors," Blancanales noted.
"Lots of motorcycles. That's where all the Outlaws
are."

Gadgets pointed. "They have LAAW rockets."

"Patrol on the ridge. This is Horse. Come in!
Report! Who the fuck are you?" "This is Jake again.
They're probably our guys, but what's got me won-
dering is the blond one's jacket. It looked exactly like
Blackie's. Black leather, those stars on the shoulders,
even the chrome studs on the sleeves. Just a second, I
don't hear their bikes moving about anymore. I'm going to look down the hill. Just a second...." "This
is Horse, I'm sending ten men out to check them.
Blackie's long gone. They could have taken his jacket
and bike. All Outlaws watch for three dudes on bikes
and wearing Outlaw jackets. All Outlaws—"

"Time to move." Gadgets jammed the walkie-
talkie in his pocket and engaged his motorcycle in
gear. Lyons and Blancanales sped after him.

Low-gearing down the hill as fast as he dared,
Lyons felt knives in his ribs at every bump. Fortu-
nately, less than a quarter mile later, the trail would
end at Vieudelou Street. But as they slowed to a walk
in order to ease through a steel gate, they saw four
Outlaws on Suzukis and cruising Hondas rounding

the turn from Stage Road. The Outlaws blocked their escape.

"Downhill!" Blancanales shouted. "Through town. They'll never expect it. We'll sprint south, then stop and pop an ambush."

Lyons sprayed the oncoming Outlaws with his Ingram, saw two go down. The other two pulled behind parked cars for cover, their bike engines roaring. He snapped a full magazine into the Ingram, jerked back the Harley's hand throttle. The front wheel left the asphalt.

Leaning through a long curve, they hit Crescent at sixty miles an hour, sideslipped through a sharp turn, then accelerated again. The roar of their motorcycles shredded the afternoon's anxious quiet.

At the Casino, Outlaws kicked their bikes to life and flew into the pursuit. Horse stood among the crowd of Outlaws starting their motorcycles. He counted off ten men, stopped the others.

"Only ten!" He held up his hands for quiet. "This could be a trick. Everyone back to their posts! Move it!"

An Outlaw on the south end of Crest had heard the radio calls. He saw the three bikers racing toward him. He started his bike. He intercepted the three men by matching their speed. He stayed handlebar to handlebar with them for a hundred yards until the sharp curves of Lovers' Cove forced him to fall back.

He jerked a pistol from his belt. Awkwardly aiming as he tried to control his motorcycle, he fired.

Lyons heard the bullet buzz past his head. He cranked back the accelerator, watching the Harley's tachometer red line.

The Outlaw pulled on the handlebars of his bike and speeded up in pursuit of the three impostors. Pulling close again, he sighted over the barrel of the revolver. He emptied the cylinder at the riders ahead of him.

Blancanales' back tire blew out. Struggling with the bucking machine, with instinct and strength he kept it upright. He lost half an inch of sole from his combat boots. Lyons slowed fast, his bike fishtailing and the back tire smoking. He pointed his Ingram at the lone pursuer and sprayed him. At least one 9mm slug would punch into his gut, he knew it. The Outlaw doubled over, his motorcycle drifting into the guardrail. At sixty miles an hour, the bike flipped. The Outlaw was sent hurtling into the seawall below.

Retrieving his backpack and weapons from his motorcycle's saddlebags, Blancanales ran to Lyons' Harley and jumped on. The ten Outlaws rounded the curve behind them.

"No time for that ambush!" Blancanales shouted. "Hope Gadgets knows where he's going!"

Glancing back, Gadgets had seen Blancanales' bike on its side in the road and a group of pursuing Outlaws closing fast on the Harley. With the weight of Blancanales, Lyons could not outdistance the Outlaws. Gadgets noticed the steel buildings of the seaplane terminal. He pointed and turned, Lyons turning only an instant behind him.

Weaving through fences, parked cars, rows of oil drums, Able Team blitzed through the open side door of a steel building, then screeched to a stop. Fire from the Outlaws outside hammered on the sheet steel walls, tiny points of light appearing with the impact of each bullet. Tools, cans and cables flew from that front wall.

Firing wild through the door, Lyons emptied his Ingram at the Outlaws. Car windows shattered, slugs slammed metal, Outlaws dived for cover. Lyons dragged the high sliding door closed. Bullets were still punching through. He dived for the floor, groaning.

"You hit?" Gadgets called out.

"Nah, I just hurt." Rolling onto his back, Lyons surveyed the interior of the building. It was a steel prefab, twelve feet high from the concrete floor to the corrugated metal roof. It contained a workshop and a storage area. A forklift stood against the far wall. A row of 50-gallon oil drums lined another wall. Crates, tires, and seaplane pontoons crowded one end of the building. Small windows viewed the ocean on one side, the terminal on the other. The door Lyons had just closed was the only way out. Outside, a voice called to them:

"Give up! We need hostages, not corpses. Give up or we'll kill you."

"Bad scene," Gadgets muttered.

Lyons grinned. "Real bad scene. No doubt about it."

15

Banzai directed his squad of Outlaws to encircle the steel building. He sent two men with rifles to cover the south wall. Two other men ran behind the airline offices, took positions covering the east wall and part of the north. Banzai spread out his other men throughout the parking lot and equipment yard.

Keying his walkie-talkie, he reported to Horse: "I've got men covering every way out. And there's nothing but the ocean behind them."

"Take them alive," Horse ordered.

"What if they won't come out?"

"Then kill them."

Banzai called out again to the besieged warriors. "Come out or we kill you."

An Uzi burst answered, the slugs punching into the car in front of him. Tinted glass showered him.

"KILL THEM!"

Shotguns and automatic rifles ripped the corrugated steel walls of the warehouse. Bullets and pellets tore through one side and out the other. Return fire from Able Team raked the cars in the parking lot.

Gasoline started to pour from the punctured tank of a Volkswagen. Then a tracer round hit the car and the fuel exploded. Two cars to the side, an Outlaw broke cover to escape the flames. Slugs caught him in

one knee and in his gut. It knocked him down. The
spreading pool of flame enveloped him. Screaming,
his body burning, the Outlaw clawed at the asphalt,
trying to drag himself clear, but without success.
Foul, greasy smoke rose from the flaming man.

Several other cars exploded. Smoke from the tires
of the already gutted Volkswagen darkened the sky.
The heat from the burning cars drove the Outlaws
out of the south end of the parking lot, leaving the
west end of the warehouse uncovered. Three bikers
gathered around Banzai.

"Ace!" Banzai looked to a man with an M-16.
"Run up that slope across the road. Put some shots
down on that end. Watch that window there." Banzai pointed to the end of the building nearest the
flaming cars.

"On my way." Ace ran through the swirling
clouds of smoke. Overweight and out of condition,
the smoke around him acrid, he panted across the
road and struggled to run up the steep embankment.
A three-shot burst broke his back, spraying parts of
him onto the crumbling rock. His broken spine
arched over in an impossible backbend. He lay in
the road, his body bent back at a ninety degree
angle.

The other two Outlaws looked at the crumpled Ace
and turned to Banzai, fear in their eyes. Banzai
pointed to a skinny man with an eyepatch.

"You, Bone. You can run fast. Make it up that
slope."

"But I only got a shotgun."

"So pick up Ace's rifle and ammo. Move it!"

"How can I run fast and pick up that stuff, too?"

he pleaded. "Besides, I can't hardly see out of this one eye of mine—"

"Can you see this?" Banzai put a .44 Magnum to Bone's face. "Now move it!"

Slinging his shotgun over his back, Bone darted from the parking lot and sprinted across the road. He snatched at the M-16 of the dead biker. The sling tangled with the dead man's arm. Bone tugged at it desperately, dragging the body to the curb before the sling pulled free.

A slug smashed Bone's right knee. He spun backwards onto the embankment, screaming. He held his knee as blood gushed between his fingers, and yelled at the others:

"I'm hit! I can't run, get me out of—"

Another slug slammed him back. "Get me out of here, ohhhhhhhhhhh—"

Then his left shoulder exploded. Both arms hung limp, blood pouring from the sleeves of his jacket. Another slug bounced him off the embankment. Yet another slug hit the gore that had been his right shoulder. Thrashing like a fish, he rolled into the road and then lay on his belly, yelping.

Banzai sighted over the eight-inch barrel of his .44 Magnum and fired a shot into Bone's head. The slug flipped the broken biker onto his back. He lay bloodied against the curb, arms and broken legs akimbo. The vast hole where his face had been stared back at Banzai.

Keying his walkie-talkie again, Banzai's voice shook: "Horse. We need rockets. Send another bunch of guys with some rockets. We need—"

"What the fuck's going on!" the voice screamed

from the radio. "You got them trapped. Now you need rockets? What kind of jerk-off are you? You got grenades, use them!"

"We still need more men. I've lost three guys already. We need the rockets to knock down the building."

"Okay, they're on their way. Use your grenades, rip the place up. The rockets will be there in four minutes."

Pulling a fragmentation grenade from his jacket pocket, Banzai crept up between two parked cars. He motioned the biker behind him to follow. The biker carried an antique Thompson submachine gun with a drum magazine.

"Put a burst in there when I stand up to throw. I'll tell you when." He watched the warehouse door, now open six inches. A muzzle flashed fire. Another weapon fired from one of the small windows. Banzai jerked the pin from the grenade. "Okay, right now!"

The biker behind Banzai stood up and fired the Thompson, which jumped awkwardly in his hands. He waved the muzzle back and forth, the .45 caliber slugs crumpling the thin corrugated metal of the warehouse.

Banzai swung his arm back to throw. The biker behind him fired the clumsy Thompson point-blank into the back of his head.

"Jesus, Banzai! I'm sorry!"

The live grenade fell at the fool biker's feet, then rolled under the car. In panic he dropped to his hands and knees, grabbing for the grenade. It rolled beyond his reach. He stood up; slugs ripped past his head. He reached for his Thompson. Suddenly the grenade exploded, shockingly fierce; it tore away both his feet, also the hand grasping the Thompson.

The mutilated man fell to his knees almost on top of the mangled body of Banzai. More slugs punched into the cars. In shock and panic, the biker rose again and staggered backward on his shortened legs. He fell in the center of the parking lot, wailing, blood spurting from the stumps of his legs and wrist.

Firing from behind an oil drum, a biker with a braided beard heard the grenade explode. Squinting through the thick, stinking smoke, he saw a shadow fall back screaming. He called out:

"Banzai! Hey, you all right?" There was no answer. Slugs pounded the 50-gallon steel drum. Oil drained from the many bullet holes. "Banzai!"

Still without an answer, the biker squatted low against the drum. He jammed shells into the tube of his riot shotgun. He came to the end of his bandolier. He had eight shots in his shotgun, three more in the loops of his bandolier. Then he had only his Browning Double-Action. "Banzai," he screamed again. "You hit?"

Leaning out from behind the oil drum, the biker pumped three loads of double-ought pellets into the warehouse door. Then he broke cover and ran weaving and ducking through the equipment yard. He was sprinting for the line of parked cars just barely visible in the pall of burning tires and cars. A 9mm slug tripped him, sending him rolling. He crawled the last few feet.

Blood oozed from his boot. He had a through-and-through wound to his ankle. Behind the protective bulk of a parked pickup, he tried to slip off his

heavy boot. He leaned back against the car, panting
with pain. He saw a radio lying on the asphalt,
probably Banzai's. He reached for it.

"Calling Horse, this is the Frog. I think Banzai's
dead. We need help, man. We're all ripped to shit. I
don't know who these crazies are, but they're doing it
to us. Send us some artillery. I'm almost out of ammo...."

He smelled gasoline. He noticed the car and truck
on each side of him sat on their wheel rims, the tires
blown apart. Streams of gasoline and oil puddled the
asphalt all around the biker.

"... I got to get out of here. I'm sitting in gasoline.
Get us some help. I'm shot. I only hear two or three
guys still shooting. Horse! Get us some help!"

Putting the radio in his pocket, the biker crawled
between the cars. He heard a single rifle slug whap
through the car beside him. A tracer flashed by his
face like a streak of fire.

The gasoline beneath him burst into flame.

Motorcycles roared around the curve at Lover's
Cove and accelerated on the straightway. Approaching the seaplane terminal, the thick smoke forced
them to slow. The five bikers heard only sporadic firing. As they pulled into the parking lot, stopping far
from the burning cars, they saw something run toward them.

A flaming Outlaw was staggering, thrashing,
lurching through the smoke. His eyes were gone, his
open mouth a hole of darkness from which came an
animal groan.

Charlie pulled his pistol and fired twice into the
faceless head. Then Charlie himself flew back, a

stream of .308 slugs ripping across his chest. Merciless engagement.

High in the corrugated steel warehouse, near the roofline, a muzzle kept flashing, the points of light bright through the black sooty smoke. The newly arrived bikers had only time to lift their eyes toward the M-60 before the slugs found them. Inaccurate because of the smoke, the stream of slugs sought no targets. The machinegunner simply swept the fire over them, firing indiscriminately.

The .308 slugs smashed knees and skulls, punched holes through the motorcycles, tore through lungs and hearts to destroy the fiberglass LAAW rocket tubes slung across the Outlaws' backs. Slugs pocked the asphalt, found flesh, ricocheted from engine blocks.

One biker, as a slug shattered his leg, threw himself sideways and dragged himself out of the kill zone. He watched as the steady stream of slugs stitched across the parking lot again and again, shooting the dead all over again, spilling entrails, giving corpses sudden movement.

The biker braced himself and struggled to remove the LAAW rocket from his back. He was almost unconscious from his leg's pain. Every move brought agony like he'd never known. He heard shrieking, did not realize his own throat made the sounds. But he got the rocket off his back.

The M-60 had quit. From the area around the warehouse, a shotgun fired: one shot, two shots, then a pause.

Laying still on his back, the one surviving biker from Charlie's rescue squad struggled to deal with the LAAW rocket's extension tube. Finally he pulled it out, and saw the sight flip up.

He heard boots running toward him. He saw above him an Outlaw holding an assault rifle. But his vision swam, he could not recognize the Outlaw's face.

"Just in time," said the Outlaw standing above him. "We've been waiting for the rockets."

"Here," the biker gasped, offering the LAAW rocket.

The Outlaw carefully accepted the ready-to-fire rocket launcher.

"Kill them!" the dying biker spat, his limp hands splashing in his own warm blood. "They killed Charlie, they killed our brothers.... Waste those bastards...." His voice faded.

"Ready?" The Outlaw above him spoke into a radio.

A voice squawked, "All clear."

Putting the rocket launcher to his shoulder, the Outlaw sighted on the far end of the warehouse, and fired.

Screeching into the smoke, the rocket hit and passed through the corrugated steel like paper, punching through the hurriedly stacked crates, the sheet metal and thick planking offering only enough resistance to detonate the warhead. Twelve ounces of Octol high explosive ripped apart the stacked drums of oil and the cans of gasoline, vaporizing the oil and the fuel.

The door and windows flying out, the warehouse became a single ball of flame. Anyone inside would die before feeling pain, instantly incinerated. Twisted sheets of steel floated upward in the flames.

Shielding his face from the flash, the standing Outlaw watched the warehouse disintegrate, then squatted beside the biker. But the biker was dead, drained of blood.

The Outlaw put the expended launcher tube on the biker's chest, folding his hands around it.

Then the Outlaw slipped away into the swirling smoke. Motorcycles roared to life, moved on out.

16

Wind tangled his hair with his beard. Horse surveyed the devastation and death. The warehouse still burned. Smoke poured from the shell of buckled, scorched sheet steel. Gutted hulks of cars smoldered in the parking lot, wisps of acrid matter drifting from blackened interiors.

At the entrance to the parking lot, Horse looked down at Charlie's annihilated squad. The four Outlaws were sprawled amongst the wreckage of their motorcycles. Their ripped bodies had stiffened in the postures of death: hands knotted over spilled viscera, faces contorted in agony as if they still screamed. A pool of oil, gasoline and coagulated blood added background color to the group.

Twenty feet to one side, a dead man embraced the tube of the expended LAAW rocket.

"Last thing he did," Stonewall said.

Without commenting, Horse strolled on. He looked down at the scabs, bones, greasy meat that had once been an Outlaw. He observed closely the eight-inch barrel of the revolver lying in ash.

"That was Banzai," he said. "I gotta talk to Turk."

Stonewall called to a group of bikers standing near the burning warehouse. "Turk! Horse here wants to talk to you."

The balding giant plodded over to his commander. Turk carried a riot shotgun slung over his back. Only two 12-gauge cartridges remained in the bandolier that crossed his chest.

"Where were you?" Horse asked him.

"I was over there." Turk pointed to a seawall on the far side of the airline terminal. "Hanging my ass over the water, covering the big door and the side facing the water."

"Did any of them get away?"

"Nothing got out. Banzai had us surround the place. Guys on the other side, guys on these sides, me covering that end. We kept shooting until the rocket hit it. And bang, it went up."

"They're not even shit now," Stonewall said, looking at the warehouse.

"Just smoke," said Turk.

"It ain't funny!" Horse's eyes were fit to kill. "We lost twelve brothers. You understand? Those locals took twelve of us with them."

Turk backed away as Horse brought up his MAC-10. "Horse, easy man. I was here. It was bad, man, it was bad! But we won. We offed them. Take it easy."

Turning his back on Turk, Horse walked to the warehouse. He shielded his face against the heat and moved closer to the red hot wall of the warehouse. He snatched up a cartridge casing and an odd bit of metal from the concrete.

"What's that?" Stonewall called to him.

"A .308 casing and a belt link for an M-60."

"No wonder they ripped our dudes up. They had a goddamned machine gun. Where the fuck did they—"

"From Chief. He had one of the M-60's. These

were the locals who got the Chief. And all of Chief's men. And the Monk. And the twelve men here. Heroes. Thinking they're going to save the day, screw up our plan, protect the wife and punk kids—"

Horse angrily threw the cartridge casing and belt link into the flames. He spoke to the rising column of smoke. "This is it, heroes. You killed my men, I killed you. But that payback ain't enough. Now I'll kill your people! All of your people!"

He laughed eerily, his gaunt addict's face cavernous like the skull in flames on his jacket's insignia.

"I wonder who they were?" Roger Davis said, rewrapping his shot-through forearm. He drew the strip of hotel sheet tight and tucked in the end. He tried to make a fist, but winced from the pain.

"Whoever they were," Chris told him, "they took out a lot of creeps."

From the roof of the hotel, the youths could see only the smoke from the burning terminal. But they had monitored the pursuit and battle on the captured walkie-talkie.

"If everyone had fought like them," Roger said as he looked into the distance, "the Outlaws wouldn't have lasted ten minutes. But everyone just did what they were told—"

"The Outlaws tricked everyone, people didn't know. Only people who didn't follow instructions got away. Like us. Like Mr. and Mrs. Shepard. Like those three guys."

"Wonder who they were. . . ." He turned to Chris. "What'll you do if they spot us? If they try to take us?"

"I saw what they did to those old people. That's what they'll try and do with us. But in these jackets—" he pointed to the bloodstains on the denim "—with rifles and pistols and all the stuff that we took from their guys, oh man, we don't have any choices. We fight. That's all there is."

"Here they come!" Roger hissed. The roar of motorcycles announced the return of the Outlaws from the Pebbly Beach seaplane terminal.

Drawing their heads down as the Outlaws passed, both boys tightened their grip on their weapons: Chris holding the M-14, Roger a revolver in his left hand. They had counted only five bikers.

They looked up again, saw the bikers continue to the Casino. Chris grinned. "Not as many as there used to be."

Shirley pressed through the Ballroom's crowd. A child pulled at her sweatsuit. She leaned down, listened to the little girl, then took the girl's hand. She walked with her to the edge of the huge circle of residents in the center of the dance floor.

"Joe, Andy," she called out. Two wide-shouldered men turned. "This little girl—what's your name, honey?"

"Georgia, like the state."

"Well, gentlemen. Please escort Miss Georgia to the little girl's room. She's afraid to go with just her mother."

The shorter, stronger man glanced to the Outlaw guarding the exit door near the women's restroom. "I know the story. We'll take her over." Then he leaned close to Shirley: "Notice there's only one of them at each door now? What's happened outside?"

"I don't know. Something."

Joe smiled slightly, then he and the second man walked with the young girl across the expanse of dance floor.

Shirley continued on to Max Stevens. A teenage boy was speaking with Max.

"Why would they need gasoline? You think they're going to make a break for it in a boat? Maybe a plane?"

"Who knows? But thank you for reporting, try to hear something whenever you think it's safe. Shirley, just a minute. Mr. Andrews over here has been waiting to tell me—yes, Mr. Andrews?"

The elderly man in red silk smoking robe and leather slippers told his story:

"...I kept my legs up. He came into the restroom and walked along the toilet stalls checking to see which ones were empty. I had my legs up, and he went into the stall next to me. What he said, I listened to every word: 'Horse, this is your friend. Have you eliminated...good. The loss of your men is unfortunate. Horse, understand this, it is the threat of action against the hostages that keeps the authorities at a distance. You do not need an army to defend the island. The threat is your defense. After we board the submarine, the survival of these petty bourgeoisie'— that is what he said—'the survival of these petty bourgeoisie is immaterial. We will have the gold, we will have our escape, do as you will....' Then he said he'd talk with him again soon and he left. I waited until my legs couldn't goddamn take it any more, then I came out. He never saw me."

"Good. Good," Max told the elderly man. "Thank you."

An Outlaw had entered the Ballroom while the old man was speaking. The Outlaw went to one of the emergency fire hoses, opened the glass-doored compartment, and twisted the valve inside. A mere trickle of water dripped from the brass nozzle of the hose. Then he twisted the valve closed.

The Outlaw glanced at the sixteen hundred prisoners crowding the center of the Ballroom. A hideous smirk distorted his face. Then he left.

Fear struck Max like a wave.

The sun fell behind the mountains to the west of Avalon. Autumn chill was arriving with the dusk shadows, and Chris and Roger Davis pulled their Outlaws jackets tight around them. A motorcycle passed on Crescent. Roger snuck a glance over the edge of the hotel's roof to the street below. The biker carried a five-gallon red and yellow can.

"More gasoline," Roger said.

"We got to tell Mr. Shepard. Maybe he can think of some way to warn... Keep listening, maybe...."

Chris took the stairs down to the third floor, and he went into one of the rooms. The bed squeaked in the room.

"Mr. Shepard, it's Chris."

Glen Shepard got to his feet wearing only his pants. But he held his sawed-off riot shotgun. Chris saw huge bruises on his ribs and chest.

"Roger and I, we've been listening to the walkie-talkie and watching the street." Chris motioned Glen to follow him. Glen picked up his Outlaws jacket and put it on as they went to the roof.

"We can't believe what we think is happening. They had a roll call on the radio, and hardly anybody answered. This Horse guy keeps calling names, and the bikers say, 'Haven't seen him in hours,' 'Don't know where he went,' stuff like that. Then Horse starts screaming about 'payback for the brothers, burn these locals.' He sent his men out for gasoline. That's all they've been doing for hours."

"Gasoline?" Glen asked. "How much gas does a motorcycle use?"

"It's not for the motorcycles."

Roger had the walkie-talkie pressed to his ear. "Listen...."

"Got it drained?" the radio said. "Still coming out. Down to drops now—" "Put the cap back on. We can't wait all—" "Mustn't have any water in the line." "Cap it off! Upstairs, you guys there? Upstairs!" "Stand-pipe's empty." "Okay then. A little water in the pipes wouldn't matter, when that gas comes out of the fire hose and the fire sprinklers, a little water won't slow it down a bit. This is going to be one hot ballroom, hot time on the old town tonight—" Laughter.

Roger started to his feet. "Now we know."

"They took a car to the gas station, just kept going back and forth with cans," Chris told Glen Shepard. "They must have hundreds of gallons of it. Hundreds."

Glen nodded. "They said 'fire hose and the fire sprinklers.' They'll need a few gallons, that's for sure."

Chris spoke with panic in his voice. "They've turned the building into a bomb. My mom and dad are in there, Roger's mom, everybody in our family, everybody we know in town, all those people—"

"What can we do, Mr. Shepard?" Roger asked him.

Looking up at the darkening sky, Glen watched the gulls gliding on the wind. High above the dusk-shadowed town, the gulls still flew in sunlight, their wings white against the violet sky. He swept his eyes over the mountains, drinking in the thousand shades of green, brown, blue, the points of yellow wild flowers, the red flowers of hillside homes. What a beautiful island, he thought. He had moved to Catalina because it was a small town set in a desert paradise isolated by the ocean. He had wanted to walk with his children on the island's beaches and mountains, through its desert wilderness and gardens of tropical flowers. Now his child would walk without a father.

"How old are you two?" he asked the Davis cousins.

"Eighteen," Chris answered.

"Sixteen, seventeen next month," Roger told him.

"So you're drafted. I want you to write your parents letters, tell them what happened today, tell them that you loved and respected them, and that there was no one else to help. You had to."

"What're we going to do?" Roger asked.

Across the bay, the Casino's automatic lights came on. The light bathed the white building in brilliance. Chris and Roger saw Glen Shepard staring, turned to see what he watched. Chris spoke first:

"We're going over there?"

"We have to. There's nobody else. I'll be back in a few minutes." Then Glen left to say goodbye to his wife.

17

"Voice-graph analysis confirms voice of gang collaborator as that of John Severine, atomic theoretician and suspected Soviet agent. Capture of Severine considered highest priority—"

"But what about the people?" Lyons demanded of the recorded voice. "Didn't you Federals get the message?"

"Sssh!" Gadgets silenced him.

"—Concerning the peril of hostages, consensus here is that coordinated assault must be reserved for last resort. That is, if your team fails. Group here has confidence in your team. Group does not believe helicopters supposedly carrying gold to island but actually bringing airborne assault units would succeed. Solution to peril is infiltration, not external assault. Will stand by for communication."

Only their whispers and the tiny red point of the scanner/auto-recorder's power light revealed Able Team's presence in the lush hillside garden. After slipping from the warehouse under cover of the smoke and confusion, the three men—the older one, mature and mellow in his strength, the blond one, all action and intensity, but graceful, and the youngest, the tousled-haired thinking man, funny and resourceful and also very strong—had commandeered three motorcycles and retreated to the hills above the town as dusk fell. They hid behind a palatial home on the slope of Mount Ada. The terraced garden viewed Avalon, the bay, and the Casino.

They had monitored both the gang's communications and the private conversations of Horse with Severine, and they knew the full horror of the gang leader's intentions.

Though they had defeated the Outlaws at the seaplane terminal, Able Team felt no pride. They realized that Horse would take his revenge on the innocent townspeople and tourists of Avalon.

Lyons addressed his colleagues. "If I have to watch sixteen hundred innocent people die in flames, I tell you, I'm jumping off this hill. I'd rather die than see that gas bomb down there go up."

"Yeah," Gadgets nodded. "That's it. Jump off the hill."

"Hey, man," Lyons snapped back, "I know it's melodramatic, but that's how I feel. This gasoline trick, turning a whole building into a bomb, all those people—"

"Carl, I'm not being sarcastic," Gadgets said quickly. "There's a hang-glider shop in Avalon. I saw it when we were cruising—"

"Wizard! You are a wizard!" Lyons jumped to his feet, then gasped from the pain in his ribs. Clutching at the agony in his chest, he started down to the motorcycles. He looked back to them. "Come on, we got a flight to catch!"

Descending the hotel stairs silently, the Davis cousins heard Mrs. Shepard's voice. They glanced to each other. Chris reached for the fire door's handle, but Roger stopped him. "Let them be alone."

Glen Shepard soon pushed open the fire door, and was startled when he saw the boys there. His shotgun jerked up instinctively. He relaxed when he recognized them. "Ready to go?"

They nodded. "We got everything we need," Chris said as they descended the stairs.

They approached the fire door to the lobby. The hotel's timer-controlled lights were on. Glen gave instructions. "Act like rough-tough Outlaws, walk straight through."

They carried their weapons casually and crossed the bright lobby. Beyond the windows, the streetlights lit Crescent to daylight brilliance. They stepped through the service door and continued to the alley behind the hotel.

In the alley's darkness, Glen spoke to the youths once more: "All you two need to do is drive. Wait for my signal, then drive. We'll need a big truck and a fast car."

"How will you get into the Casino?"

"I'll go up Chimes Tower Road, then cut across the hills. When I'm ready to start down the hill, I'll signal you. You wait fifteen minutes, then drive for the Casino. Fire a few shots out the window to get their attention. They'll shoot at you.

"Two hundred yards from the Casino, wreck the truck so it blocks the road. Hit it with a molotov cocktail, run back to the car and split.

"Go up Marilla to Vieudelou, as if you're taking the road out of town. But turn onto La Mesa and park. Just like one of the neighborhood cars. They won't catch you, and I'll be in the Casino."

"You're just going to walk in?" Chris asked.

"Look at me! Outlaw jacket, dirty jeans, shotgun, two days' beard on my face, and I stink. I know I'll get in."

"What if—"

"What if nothing. It's the only way I can think of that any of us has any chance to do something and still live. Once I'm in, I'll do what I can."

Glen went to the alley mouth and looked up and down the side street. He whispered to the cousins. "Let's get in gear. We got to steal the truck and the car for you both. And a flashlight for me, a big one."

"Mr. Shepard, wait." Chris pulled Glen into a shadowy doorway. The teenager's eyes scanned the street for Outlaws. "Are you sure you don't want to wait for the police? Because. . . because you're going to die. I know you are."

Twisting away, Glen walked into the street. He glanced at the shop signs, started toward a hardware store. The cousins ran to catch up with him. Passing a mailbox, he pointed. The teenagers dropped in letters, then followed Glen Shepard through the dark, deserted street.

"Outlaws!" Gadgets hissed.

Stepping through the door of the ManBird Hang-Glider shop, lock-pick still in his hand, Lyons froze. Gadgets eased up his Uzi. Blancanales pushed the Uzi down, slipped out the silent Beretta.

Across the street, three Outlaws—two of them carrying shotguns, the third an M-14 rifle—crept up to a one-ton delivery truck. One Outlaw scanned the street, sawed-off riot shotgun in his hands, then tried the truck's door. Locked.

Glass shattered. On the curb side, an Outlaw opened the door, then slid across to the driver's seat. The truck's hood popped open.

Slow and silent as a shadow, Blancanales stepped back into the hang-glider shop's doorway. Taking a marksman stance, he held the Beretta in both hands and sighted on the third Outlaw. Blancanales flicked the burst selector down to single-shot.

The biker stepped behind the truck, spoke with the Outlaw sitting in the cab. The Outlaw carrying the riot shotgun slung the weapon over his shoulder and reached under the hood of the truck. The Outlaw in the driver's seat got out, closed the truck door softly, glanced toward the beach.

Blancanales pointed the Beretta at the center of this biker's forehead. He looked past the biker. He would fire when the third Outlaw was in the open. He would kill all three before they knew what hit them.

It was then that he realized that this Outlaw was only a teenager. Shaved, wearing a clean shirt under his Outlaw jacket, the boy wore filthy Levi's that bagged around his slim legs. He also wore clean tennis shoes.

"Kill them," Gadgets whispered.

The teenage Outlaw was crossing the street. He went to a curbside tree only two steps from Blancanales. The teenager leaned back against the truck and watched the street. His back was to the doorway where Able Team hid.

Silently, Blancanales stepped up behind the teenager, cupped his left hand over the boy's mouth, put the Beretta's suppressor behind his ear. Blancanales whispered to the boy:

"I'm the police. Are you an Outlaw?"

The boy shook his head, no. Blancanales took his hand off the teenager's mouth, then grabbed the M-14 he held.

"Are they Outlaws?"

"No," Chris Davis gulped.

Turning, Chris found himself face to face with what looked like a hard-eyed biker. "Glen! Roger!" Chris screamed as he punched the biker again and again. The biker locked an arm around Chris' throat. Blancanales thought, I'm getting too old for these fun and games. He held the teenager tight as the boy struggled and called out:

"Run! Run for it! They got—"

Throwing himself behind a parked car, Glen jerked the riot shotgun from his shoulder and pointed it at the shadows and dark doorways across the street. Blancanales commanded:

"Don't shoot! We're police! We got Outlaw jackets just like you. Nobody shoot!"

He stepped from the darkness, his arm locked around Chris' neck. He went to the center of the street, then released Chris. He returned the M-14 to Chris and, slipping a long-barreled automatic into his belt, removed his Outlaws jacket.

He wore a roll-necked black nylon uniform that was criss-crossed with equipment belts and magazine bandoliers. This man had no badge and Glen had never seen the uniform before, but whoever he was, he was official. Glen put the shotgun down on the sidewalk and shook hands with the black-clad officer:

"Thank God you're here. What took you so long?"

Shoving through the massed citizens of Avalon, Max Stevens assembled his resistance workers. He jerked a man away from his wife and teenage children. "Go to the other side, we're meeting. It's an emergency!" He didn't stop to answer the man's questions.

Stumbling over a sleeping mother, Max grabbed the arm of a worker gossiping with one of her spies. "Forget that, it's too late! Go to the meeting—" He pointed across the crowd, then hurried on to the next worker and the next and next. He saw Mike Carst and called out:

"Mr. Carst! Join us please. This is imperative."

Limping into the center of the assembled group, Max raised his hands for quiet.

"This morning, we agreed we would be in great danger if we attempted to escape. We agreed we would wait until the police attacked. But things have changed. Regardless of what we do now, we are at all times in great danger. Whether or not the ransom is paid, they plan to kill us all right here."

A hundred voices questioned him simultaneously. He shouted: "Quiet! Quiet! We have no choice now. We must act. We must rush those doors, or else we all die. They have filled the emergency fire sprinklers with gasoline—this entire building is a bomb. We are the explosive. They're going to hose us down and ignite us. The building, us—we all blow together—biggest bomb ever—''

Max had noticed that the man next to Mike Carst was the one he'd seen murder the Secret Service agent. That was the man who'd spoken by radio with the Outlaws, who did not care too much about the "petty bourgeoisie" of Catalina. Max decided to channel the fury of his fellow citizens toward the traitor, to distract them.

"He's a spy of the Outlaws!" he yelled, pointing at the startled individual. "He has a radio in his pocket. Grab him. Make him tell us what the Outlaws plan to do! Grab him!"

John Severine struggled to escape. But thirty men and women had seized him. He punched at them and kicked. But they were hammering him with fists, and they knocked him to the floor and held him down.

"Here's the radio! He was a spy!"

They dragged the bloodied, dazed Severine to Max. Watching from the side, young Jack Webster saw Max take a Colt automatic from under his jacket and slam the traitor across the face. His nose spurted blood.

"Spy! Murderer! You would have burned us alive, now tell us when they plan to do it! *When*?"

Jack Webster broke from the crowd and ran for the exit. Behind him, he heard Max call to him: "Stop. Jack, stop."

He ran to the lone Outlaw guarding the exit. He screamed: "Help me, they're going to kill me. They're going to rush you and break out. Tell Horse I've got names. I've got names!"

18

A cool, moist breeze from the bay made the plastic of the hang-glider's wings snap and ripple. In his roll-necked blacksuit, Lyons gripped the crossbar. He glanced up at the aluminum struts.

"You don't have to do this," Gadgets told Lyons. "It was my idea. Look at you, man, you can hardly breathe—"

"On my way. Stand back."

"Let Pol give you some local for your ribs—"

"Forget that. Half hour from now, I'll be relaxing in a hot tub. Take some pain killers yourself and relax! Hey, Politician," Lyons called.

On his belly at the edge of the clearing, Blancanales was watching the Outlaws below. Spread-eagled out on either side of him, Glen Shepard and the two teenagers listened as Blancanales pointed out their targets. He left them, went to Lyons.

"So is it clear?"

"Sure you don't want me or Gadgets to make the jump?"

"Either of you ever hang-glided?" he asked. "I have. Take my word for it, this isn't a beginner's hill. Do they know their targets?"

"Yes," confirmed Blancanales. "I'll take Glen Shepard, the teenagers will go with Gadgets. We'll leave them on the hillside, and they'll cover the road when we rush the Casino. Glen Shepard had Advanced Infantry school. He'll use the Starlite.

"They'll hold their fire until the shooting starts. They'll kill everything with an Outlaws jacket. Those three are motivated fighters—they hate those psychos. Told me if we wanted to take prisoners, we'd have to go it alone."

"And Severine won't be dressed like a biker," pointed out Lyons, still testing his grip. "So we've got a chance to take him. Gadgets, what about the Feds?"

"LAPD assault teams are in the helicopters, ready to go. Just in case."

"Great."

"Good luck, mister," one of the teenagers called out.

Lyons waved, smiling at the man with the broken teeth who seemed to be responsible for the boys.

He quickly checked the gear strapped to him—his shoulder-holstered Magnum, the silenced Beretta, the Ingram, and his combat knife. Then he began his sprint against the light breeze. Lyons did not stop running until his feet pedalled in the air.

Airborne! Soaring, the wind rushing against him, he kept his eyes on the center of the Casino roof three hundred feet below him. Crosswind carried him sideways. He leaned into the wind, pain searing his ribs. He ignored it, braced for the impact as the roof rushed up at him at remarkable speed.

He landed, very gently, and tried to run but had to double over with the agony that tore at his ribs. He hit the roof with his shoulder. He lay there gasping for a moment, the glider akimbo above him. Forcing himself to his feet, he carried the clumsy hang-glider to the turret, lashed the crossbar to one of the terra cotta columns to keep it out of the way, and pulled his combat knife.

Beer cans and cigarette butts littered the turret. Lyons smelled urine. Stepping carefully through the trash, he tried the access door. The knob turned.

Steel stairs led down. Dim fluorescent lights illuminated a cavernous area crowded with huge air conditioning and heating units. Creeping down the stairs, he smelled gasoline. He scanned the maintenance area. In an aisle between machines, he saw piled gasoline cans. A voice squawked from a walkie-talkie.

Moving silently but fast, Lyons approached the noise. He peeked around a machine and saw the shoulder of an Outlaws jacket. The walkie-talkie lay on a crate. A tank eight feet high bore the stenciled identification: EMERGENCY RESERVOIR/FIRE SPRINKLERS/BALLROOM. A ladder leaned against the tank.

He came up behind the Outlaw slowly, holding his knife low. Then he saw that the jacket was hung over an empty chair. Lyons heard boots behind him.

As the machete came down, Lyons stepped aside, guiding the long blade past him with a touch of the combat knife. He whirled and literally stepped into the biker, jamming his knee into the man's down-thrusting arm, breaking the elbow backward. Simultaneously he chopped him in the throat with his left hand, then grabbed him and threw him down on the back of his head.

Lyons collapsed against the emergency reservoir, panting for breath, fire in his ribs twisting his body.

The Outlaw was struggling to pull a pistol with his flopping arm. Lyons lunged forward and stomped the man in the throat. The Outlaw's face turned blue. The double attack on his throat had killed him.

"Mack!" the walkie-talkie called. "Turn on the pump and get down here. These people are rushing us."

Lyons keyed the radio. "Doing it!"

Finding the valve and pump, he closed the valve, then jimmied off the conduit connected to the pump motor, cut the wires. Defused the bomb.

He put on the Outlaws jacket and rushed down to the ballroom.

Creeping down the dark hillside, the teenagers in position behind him, Gadgets heard a buzz in his earphone. For silence, he had plugged this plastic earphone into the Outlaw walkie-talkie he carried. The voice screamed in his ear:

"Mack! Turn on the pump and get down here. These people are rushing us." A voice answered, "Doing it!"

The voice of Horse blared. "Everyone to the ballroom. They think they're going to rush the doors."

Across the road, the three Outlaws guarding the Casino entry rushed inside. Gadgets keyed his hand-radio. "Now, Politician. We got to get up to the ballroom, now! Lyons didn't make it—"

Both of them broke from the brush, sprinted to the entry.

Throwing the doors open, Horse entered, Stonewall on his right, Turk on his left. Other Outlaws followed. The bayonet of his shotgun fixed, Stonewall sneered at the wall of townspeople. The crowd closed ranks, a shoulder-to-shoulder wall of men and women facing the bikers.

Other doors flew open, bikers entering, weapons ready. The murmuring crowd fell quiet. Fifty feet of open floor separated the ranks of the prisoners from the Outlaws near the doors.

"Back, sheep," Horse shouted. "You miserable creatures. Which one of you is Max Stevens?"

No one answered.

"Which one of you?"

Horse went to the emergency fire hose and pulled it from its compartment. He motioned a biker over. "Turn on the valve when I tell you."

Horse walked toward the people, the hose unfolding from the rack. "Okay, Mr. Leader of the Sheep, whoever you are—come out or I spray everyone here with gasoline. Then whump! Up you all go!"

In the crowd, Mrs. Stevens gasped. She held her husband. The friends and neighbors around Max, the resistance workers he had organized, all looked to him.

"You see?" his wife cried. "You see what—"

"Quiet, Carol." He kissed her as she cried, and he slipped the pistol and spare magazine to her. Then he pushed through the crowd.

His fisherman friend tried to stop him. "Max, give us the word!" he whispered hoarsely. "We'll make our break right now!"

Twisting away from his friend, Max stepped into

the open and walked toward his death. He stopped ten feet from Horse.

Horse's heroin-ravaged face sneered. "Hero! Remember me? I'm George Delaney. I lived here. Assholes like you chased me out, sent me to prison. Now I'm going to torch you. And in a while, I'll burn the rest of them."

Signaling the biker at the valve, Horse pointed the brass fire nozzle at Max Stevens. After seconds, Horse looked at the nozzle, shook it. Some gasoline splashed out, splattering Horse as it trickled onto the floor.

"Turn it, open it up!" Horse shouted.

"It is!"

Gasoline drained from the hose. The stream never got farther than a few inches from the nozzle. Gasoline puddled around Horse.

"Fuck this!" He pulled his .45 auto from the holster, pulled back the hammer, screaming: "Going to spray your brains, hero, all over the—"

"NO!" Carol Stevens screamed. She raised her husband's pistol, fired, the slug almost missing Horse, only nicking his left arm. Horse spun in terror, firing his pistol down into the puddle of gas.

Framed in flames, he shrieked and wailed as a sheet of heat enveloped him. He dropped his pistol, slapping at his flaming body. Stonewall reached for him and tried to pull him free of the burning gasoline, but he fell back, his own hands flaming. He too dropped his gun.

Behind the bikers, a submachinegun ripped. Biker after biker fell. Other Outlaws ran. Horse hopped about the ballroom floor, flaming, shrieking. Stonewall was slapping out the flames on his hands. He reached for his shotgun on the floor.

But the people of Catalina Island took him. Hundreds of hands beat him, clawed him. He managed to fight back and with his tremendous strength he broke free. His face was pulpy and bleeding. He reached for his pistol. It wasn't there. He staggered backward from the advancing people. Then he ran from them.

Other bikers were not so fortunate. Fists beat them. When they fell, shoes and high heels and bare feet stomped them. Blood and pulverized flesh splashed around their broken bodies.

On the balcony ringing the Casino, Lyons ran through the Outlaws, firing point-blank bursts from his Ingram into their backs and into their guts. Ahead of him he saw an Outlaw aiming his shotgun at the crowd inside the ballroom.

Ten feet from the outlaw, Lyons fired. Only one 9mm slug hit the biker, snapping his wrist. Staggering back, the Outlaw slid his left hand down to his shotgun's trigger. Lyons pulled his Python, popped a shot through the biker's chest, the hollow-point slug throwing the dying biker actually backwards through the air.

Running past the fallen Outlaw, Lyons fired a second shot through the man's forehead, then blasted another Outlaw running for the stairs.

His shoulder suddenly in fragments, Stonewall tumbled down the stairs. But he got up, ran, his dead arm swinging by tendons and stubborn strands of muscle.

"Lyons!" A voice shouted to him. Blancanales ran to him, G-3 in his hands. "Take off that jacket!"

"Oh, yeah." Lyons ripped off the stinking denim as Blancanales fired burst after burst, the powerful auto-rifle slamming Outlaws into walls, throwing one over the balcony railing.

Methodically sweeping the balcony with his Uzi, Gadgets killed. An Outlaw was running from a group of citizens. Gadgets snapped two shots through the panicked biker's spine, then stepped over him to fire again. He moved on, putting a burst through a crawling biker's head, snapping a shot through the face of a biker reloading a shotgun. He emptied the last two rounds of the magazine through the dying shotgunner's head.

Calmly dropping the Uzi's magazine, Gadgets put it in his pocket, snapped in another, continued his search for living Outlaws. There were more than seventy when this day dawned. Not anymore.

On the hillside overlooking the Casino's entrance, Glen Shepard squinted through the strange electronics of the Starlite scope. Hearing the firing and screaming high above him on the balcony, he glanced up. But he could see nothing that happened.

A biker ran from the entry and jumped on a motorcycle. Shotgun blasts from Chris and Roger Davis, twenty yards to Glen's side, ripped the biker. Then Glen saw Stonewall run from the Casino.

"Don't shoot him!" Glen shouted to the teenagers. "He's Stonewall...."

Looking to Chris, Roger asked: "He doesn't want us to shoot him? What's going on?"

"That's the psycho who killed the old people," Chris said, sighting the M-14 on the biker's chest. "He wants him for himself."

A .308 slug snapped Stonewall's knee backward, throwing him against the steps of the Casino. Chris lowered his M-14 to watch. Twenty yards from them, Glen chambered another .308 accelerator and fired into Stonewall's other leg. Then his thigh. Then his hip. Then his uninjured arm.

On the balcony, Able Team moved through the carnage. They saw Outlaws with their heads stomped flat by the islanders. Groups of islanders were beginning to form around Able Team, touching them, shaking their hands, a hundred voices thanking them.

Lyons saw a man run. Preparing to sprint after him, a full thirty-round magazine in his Ingram, he shouted:

"Stop! Whoever you are, stop or I'll fire!"

"Don't!" A middle-aged man called from near Lyons. "It's a local boy." The man limped up to Lyons; he had a Colt Hardballer in the waistband of his slacks.

"Why's he running?" Lyons asked.

"Because he's afraid," he said, his voice sad. "And he'd better keep running, all the way to the mainland. Where they don't know him."

"Who are you?"

"Max Stevens," said the man, shaking hands with Lyons, smiling broadly. "I sell things, including homes. Despite what you see, Catalina is almost paradise—"

Shotgun blasts came from the street below the balcony. Lyons ran back to Gadgets and Blancanales. They had a bloody-faced John Severine, Soviet agent, in their grip.

"More Outlaws!" Lyons shouted, running down the stairs. He raced down flight after flight, only slowing when he came to the Casino entry. Ingram ready, he glanced outside.

Glen Shepard stood over a screaming biker. Behind Glen, the teenage boys turned their faces away from what they saw. Firing at point-blank range, Glen blew away pieces of Stonewall's body.

The legless Outlaw thrashed on the steps. Pointing the sawed-off shotgun again, Glen blew off Stonewall's left hand and forearm.

Lyons aimed his Ingram at the head of the suffering man. Glen shouted, "Don't. Let him die. I wish I could kill him a hundred times." He squatted down in front of the truncated criminal. "Hey, animal. You looked for me all day. I watched you butcher those old people. But I killed your psycho Outlaws, and I got you. Me, a restaurant manager, a guy who punches a time clock, I killed you. You hear me?"

Breath wheezing from Stonewall's throat, he died. Glen kicked the corpse. He looked down on the jacket's evil insignia.

"Forever Outlaws." Glen spat on the flaming skull.

Lyons looked down at the dead psychopath. "Forever came tonight."

EPILOGUE

Days later at Stony Man, Brognola called together the men of Able Team. "I have transcripts of the interrogation of John Severine. As suspected, he was a Soviet agent. Transcripts for all of you—"

Brognola passed inch-thick folders to Blancanales, Gadgets and Lyons. "The first page summarizes the findings. Though it was at first incredible that Severine, an atomic theoretician and respected member of his community, would conspire with Delaney, an addict and gang leader—"

"Nothing's impossible in California," Lyons commented.

"What the interrogators learned, in three days of marathon questioning, was that Severine was obsolete. Simply that. He had struggled thirty years to rise to the highest level of the American defense program. He'd appeared to be a total career man, sacrificing his personal happiness to serve his country. To his superiors and fellow theoreticians, he seemed to be the dedicated genius. And he was.

"But the advance of weapons science left him behind. He helped create the atomic weapons of the sixties and seventies. But the weapons of the future are high-energy lasers and particle beam projectors. There was no role in the development programs for him. And without that role, despite his brilliance, despite his achievements, despite the respect of his scientist peers, regulations dictated that he lose his top secret clearance.

"He apparently met with his Soviet contact in Washington DC and requested that he be withdrawn from the United States. The KGB denied his request, telling him to stay in place until his retirement.

"That gave him two choices. Stay on as an aging specialist in obsolete weapon-science. He had already put in thirty years, counting college and graduate school. Or he could defy his superiors and return to the Soviet Union. Which meant the Gulag, forced labor in Siberia until he died.

"Instead, he decided to take an American atomic submarine home. Without it, he was a defiant middle-aged spy refusing to do his duty to the State. With the submarine, he would have been a People's Hero.

"And that, gentlemen, is it. He had no interest in the gold. We thought the submarine was a way to avoid using a jetliner to escape—avoiding having to wander the airports of the world, searching for a nation that would offer sanctuary to a gang of psychopathic Americans."

"The sub would have been his ticket home," Gadgets said, "because it's a first-line weapon system. Everything new. Everything the Russians want. Wow, all that insanity that happened on Catalina was because of a graying Communist intellectual. Jeez."

"Of course," Brognola concluded, "the Soviets claim complete innocence."

"Yeah," Lyons added. "Like they don't know about Libya, or the PLO, or the Cubans. Don't know a thing about it."

Blancanales flipped through his transcript. He saw page after page of blacked-out text. Most of the pages had only a quotation or two remaining. The genial man laughed, showing the pages to the others.

"What is this? You've given us a transcript that doesn't make any sense."

"I'm sorry," Brognola told them. "But most of the matters discussed in the interrogation were top secret."

"Basically, therefore," commented Lyons, "we go cruising around in kayaks snuffing crazy dopers for the Feds and we don't get to know why."

"It's a matter of 'Need to Know,'" Brognola explained.

"Okay, Hal," Lyons grinned. "Here's something we all Need to Know. Where's Mack?"

"Colonel John Phoenix is right here, as a matter of fact," announced Brognola. "Stony Man is something of a castle for him nowadays. God knows the man deserves a home." He pressed the buzzer on his polished walnut desk. "April, the colonel is in his quarters. He'd be delighted to know that his colleagues in Able Team have arrived and been debriefed. Would you like to inform him of this, please?"

The four men chatted amiably as they waited for the big guy. It was true: everybody did Need to Know about Mack, his whereabouts and activities, however covert. He was the lifeblood of this place.

Sure, there were others close to The Executioner

who had learned to blaze truth across the chicken shit canvas of these times—The Bear, Leo, Jack Grimaldi, Able Team of course... And they did it with as much fierce courage as Mack, with the same dedication to uphold justice despite the law.

But Mack—Col. John Phoenix—was the origin of their strength. When Bolan entered, all eyes looked his way.

"Welcome, Able Team," he said, his steel eyes alive with good humor. He was wearing casual attire. "I hear you've excelled yourselves once more." He shook hands with each of the team, motioning them to stay seated as he did so. His handshake was firm, conveying very well his thanks to these men, and his respect for their fighting skills.

"It was a bed of roses," smiled Lyons.

"You are wounded, Carl," Bolan said to him. "We have good facilities for medical treatment here, in fact the best you're going to find anywhere. I should force you to stay and enjoy them."

"I'll think about it," parried Lyons. "But let me tell you, I think we'd all be dead men if Stony Man hadn't come up with that armorer guy who supplied us with the hardware."

"Konzaki," prompted Blancanales. "We owe him all a favor."

"Where'd you come up with him?" asked Gadgets.

Bolan looked at Brognola. "He's CIA, as you know," Mack said, "but I feel we'll need to continue to recruit his services, the way things are going in the world."

"He's more or less our weapon-smith now," Hal added. "You guys will be seeing a lot more of him."

"How'd he lose his legs," persisted Schwarz, always curious.

Bolan answered. "At the assault on Hue, during the Tet Offensive—he was leading his platoon to the rescue of an ambushed unit. A sniper got him four or five times in both legs.

"His men tried to pull him to cover, but Konzaki ordered them back for their own safety.

"That sniper killed two men before Konzaki threatened to shoot any other member of the platoon who disobeyed his command to abandon him."

Bolan was relaxed. The late afternoon sun warmed Hal's Stony Man study with its reddening rays. This evening would be a more than welcome respite for Mack between missions, and it would be a pause for his exhausted Able Team, these tried and true men: a large evening, full of talk, and memory. They must take advantage of it.

Blancanales set the mood. "Goddammit there are some brave people out there—"

"Think of how many men we could recruit for Stony Man," added Lyons. "Glen Shepard for one. Max Stevens." Pol and Gadgets nodded. "Those kids out on Catalina, Chris and Roger. In their own way they have more courage than any of us."

"I heard about the help you guys got, Hal was telling me," agreed Bolan. "Yeah, they are courageous. They have the courage not to see themselves as victims. I like that. They have jobs, they have complicated daily lives. But they're not up against the wall anymore."

Mack stared out the window. "You make a good point, Carl. They are more courageous than the warrior, because they are so closely attached to others, they are so vulnerable to the misfortunes of their loved ones." The big man's voice was sad, but far from resigned. "They are different from the warrior. They are not us yet.

"But they are becoming so. They are becoming so."

ABLE TEAM

AN EXECUTIONER SERIES

#1 Tower of Terror

ON SALE NOW!

Able Team—Carl Lyons, Pol Blancanales and Gadgets Schwarz—have been directed by Mack Bolan to put down terrorist outrages too volatile and unpredictable for regular law enforcement. Able Team works undercover, with deadly purpose, against the most extreme rampages of injustice.

TOWER OF TERROR is the story of an invasion of one of Wall Street's greatest skyscrapers. The tower is captured by a group of Puerto Rican psychos, armed to the teeth with weaponry purchased by means of huge sums of embezzled U.S. money. Able Team must recapture the building fast, before the public gets a chance to panic. The build-up to the assault is a series of episodes of tremendous suspense. Here are Lyons and Blancanales in just such a moment:

She hurried up the four flights of stairs, Lyons a few steps behind her. Was her supple sway deliberate? In the narrow, closed stairwell, he became aware of her perfume and sweat. He kept a tight grip on his Uzi.

At the fourth-floor fire door, she stopped and stepped closer to him, her mask of fanaticism gone, her face vulnerable, her eyes searching his face for a response. She stepped closer, her small breasts almost touching him.

"I will cooperate completely," she said.

As she snapped her knee into his groin, Lyons whipped his hips sideways to her, blocked her knee with his own. He tried to block her fists with his left hand, but took the double-hand blow to his stomach and fell back against the stair rail.

Screaming in Vietnamese, she jerked open the fire door and ran into an apartment. Lyons bounced off the railing.

He pressed himself back against the hallway wall and watched slugs splintering the apartment door. Burst after burst ripped through the door, at chest height, then at knee height, slugs gouging into the landing's linoleum.

Watching the ragged holes appear, Lyons waited until at least 30 shots had come through. Then, betting his life she had an AK-47 with a 30-round magazine, he stepped away from the wall and fired waist-high through the door.

Blancanales was watching him from the elevator. He ran up to Lyons, went to one knee, and waited.

Lyons kicked the splintered door down. Both Lyons and Blancanales fired criss-crossing bursts into the apartment.

Blancanales dived through the doorway, low, as Lyons fired over him. He heard Blancanales exchanging fire somewhere in the apartment, shots hitting the wall, breaking glass. Furniture crashed.

Lyons glanced in, saw Blancanales roll behind an overstuffed velvet couch. An Oriental man had shouldered an AK and was firing a burst.

Lyons ducked back from the doorway as shots ripped wood out of the doorframe beside his face. Then he heard the Uzi burst. The AK fire went wild. A man screamed.

Lyons looked again. The Vietnamese was gone, the window where he had stood was also gone. The afternoon breeze flagged the curtains.

Blancanales would be out of ammo by now. Then he saw Le Van Thanh aiming a pistol at him. Lyons fired at her.

The first slug punched into the wall behind her, but the second and third hit her shoulder, threw bits of flesh and cloth onto the wallpaper, and spun her violently around. She dropped to the floor. Her pistol clattered to the floor. Lyons took aim at her head, but his gun was empty.

Incredibly, she came up with an AK. Lyons was grappling with Gadgets' satchel, trying to get the unused Uzi out. The wounded woman dropped the empty magazine from the AK and tried to snap in another. She never reached the AK's cocking lever.

Lyons swung the satchel by its shoulder strap, the nylon bag heavy with Uzi and magazines, hand-radio and spent brass, coming down on her head hard, stunning her. She dropped the AK. Lyons swung the satchel again, saw blood gushing from her head, pouring over her face and white blouse.

Still she struggled, putting her hands out in front of her in kung-fu claws, kicking, but in the slow motion of semiconsciousness. Lyons dropped the satchel, took out his Colt Python .357, grabbed her by her lustrous black hair, and smashed her in the ear with the Python's heavy barrel.

Silence.

Lyons and Blancanales looked around the apartment again, surveying the damage.

It had been a spacious apartment with French windows overlooking the trees of the street. Now, most of the glass was shot out. One entire window was gone. The curtains were splattered with blood. The furnishings were ripped, broken, overturned, dusted with plaster and bits of brick. The velvet couch looked as if it had been attacked with a chain saw. Lines of automatic rounds dotted the walls, hunks of plaster breaking away from the bricks beneath.

Gadgets rushed in. "You've got to get out of here," he yelled. "There's a crowd outside, the police are on their way. We got a Vietnamese hanging out of a tree with most of his head gone. I'm afraid this is going to be on the six-o'clock news...."

ABLE TEAM
PHOENIX FORCE

These new series have been produced by Don Pendleton in the bestselling tradition of THE EXECUTIONER. Like Mack Bolan, the men of Able Team and Phoenix Force are fighters for ultimate justice, even when it has to be above and beyond the law.

Don Pendleton would like to hear from you about these books. He invites you to write to him to give your views on Mack's new avenger teams. Your response will ensure exciting new directions for Able Team and Phoenix Force, with damn fine stories to keep you reading. Write to:

Don Pendleton
c/o Gold Eagle Books
P.O. Box 22188
Tempe, AZ 85281